For K...

Africa's
Unfinished
Symphony

Lucia Mann

Africa's Unfinished Symphony

Lucia Mann

Grassroots Publishing Group, Inc.
www.GrassrootsPublishingGroup.com

GRASSROOTS PUBLISHING GROUP™
9404 Southwick Dr.
Bakersfield, California 93312
www.GrassrootsPublishingGroup.com

10 9 8 7 6 5 4 3 2
First Edition 2013
Printed in the United States of America

ISBN: 978-0-9794805-6-0
Library of Congress Control Number: 2013931168

Cover & book design by CenterPointe Media

Dedication

Africa's Unfinished Symphony is warmly dedicated to my beloved husband, Hector; my adored daughters and grandchildren; and most of all, to the African people. The power of their human spirit and courage to beat all odds provides a solid foundation of this novel.

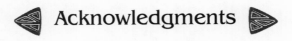

Acknowledgments

Special credit to my editor and publisher, Nesta Aharoni, whose perception, critique, and understanding make it a delight to embark on the long road between story concept and completed novel. Special acknowledgment to my proofreader, Galia Aharoni, who has been a delight to work with. And special gratitude to my readers. I am indebted to them for their support and steadfast confidence in my ability to weave the fabric of yet another inspirational African story.

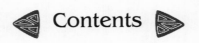

Contents

HISTORICAL FACT
~ Pretoria, South Africa, Tuesday, May 10, 1994 ~

ON THIS HISTORICAL DAY, as brilliant blue jacaranda petals stood out against a cloudy, winter sky, Rolihlahla Nelson Dalibunga Mandela was elected president of South Africa. After more than three centuries of white rule, he became the country's first black president, thus ending apartheid—the "human disaster"—the unconscionable segregation by color which had been occurring for sixty-three years.

Jubilant scenes flowed onto the streets of Pretoria. Men, women, and children of all races sang and danced with joy. Together they were celebrating a historical event, a ceremony that was taking place in the administrative capital of the Republic of South Africa.

President Nelson Mandela's message of a democratic South Africa was indisputable, as is displayed in the following excerpts from his inaugural speech, given May 10, 1994 in Pretoria:

> We saw our country tear itself apart in a terrible conflict.
> The time for healing of the wounds has come.
> Let there be justice for all.
> Let there be peace for all.
> Let there be work, bread, water, and salt for all.
> Never, never, and never again shall it be that this beautiful land will again experience the oppression of one by another and suffer the indignity of being the skunk of the world.
> *Let freedom reign.*

PROLOGUE
~ Soweto Township, Gauteng, South Africa, 1994 ~

"All human beings are born free
and equal in dignity and rights."
—*Universal Declaration of Human Rights*
(1948 – Article 1)

MANDELA'S PROFOUND DECLARATION was too late for thousands upon thousands of African people who were sold into slavery during a brutal era in British and American history. Mandela's 1994 ceremonial proclamation, *"Let freedom reign,"* was also too late for the hundreds of black men, women, and children who lost their lives in the Soweto uprising on June 16, 1976.

On that tragic day, in a hail of automatic rifle bullets racing out of white-controlled armored vehicles, high school students protesting the enforcement of "the language of the oppressor," Afrikaans, dropped dead like swatted flies onto the dirty streets of a settlement that had been set aside for blacks by the white-ruling South African government in 1931.

Soweto Township, then and now, is a place of ghosts' footsteps that represent sacrificed settlement children who will forever be heard walking the dusty roads. Among them is someone who stood out from the crowd—a restless white soul who, like the black children, has not found peace in the beyond.

CHAPTER ONE

The Province of KwaZulu, Natal—formerly Zululand—2009

"Courage mounteth with occasion."
—William Shakespeare

AT 6 A.M. ON THIS MONDAY MORNING of December 14, a fine mist shrouded the ancient burial grounds of the forcibly evacuated Tswanas tribespeople. Underneath the summer mist, dew glistened on the lips of wild orchids—flowers of the gods— creating a stunning display of brilliant red. Circling these exotic beauties, tall thorn trees, with prickly fingers opened wide, signalled the new day by emitting a series of shrill, high-pitched reverberations that sounded like a woman wailing. A flock of black, fan-tailed drongo birds perched high above in the gnarly branches. They were deathly still, waiting for the right moment to swoop up their much-anticipated breakfast: a colony of leafcutter ants whose powerful jaws were slicing snippets of yummy orchid leaves below.

Yet even in this natural, wondrous setting, something *dark* was spreading under the rising, hot sun. *Nothing* could blanket its murkiness, not even preternatural snow!

The earthquake-like rumble that travelled throughout this hilly region was sinister. At the same time and in stark contrast, a faint cry escaped from an old woman's throat. Her naked body, which was below average height, was face down in red-ochre earth. Her short arms and legs extended outward. Her stubby fingers buried themselves deep into the graveyard soil. Bits of clammy soil caked her flattened nose, small mouth, and protruding tongue, and her eyeballs, under closed lids, darted from side to side. She was frightened, as panic-stricken as a caged animal. Everything she believed in was being tested; in her mind, she was the only remaining protector of all that was sacred to her.

Now in her late seventies, her upward-slanting eyes and other characteristics of genetic abnormality were undeniable. Vimbela Imfunda carried a burden of Down syndrome. She had the intelligence of a third grader, which, to her advantage, had kept her vivaciously alive … until today. Now she felt as old as the stars and worn down with worry. Her gentle, big-hearted ways and cheerful songs were silenced. Normally, she was not shy of speaking her mind, but at this moment, only woeful, tongue-clicking laments and bleating goat sounds escaped from her larynx.

While she was prostrate on a burial mound, a sorrow like no other invaded Vimbela's pounding heart. Tears flowed profusely as her inconsolable mind ached beyond repair. She did not even flinch when ants marched in single file over her bare flesh, each carrying a small piece of foliage. To these committed herbivores, she was merely an obstacle they had to overcome in order to reach their nest.

The Caterpillar operator was fast approaching. In front of him, Vimbela loomed like the mythical hound Cerberus, guarding the gates to the underworld. She was a sitting duck. The Kenyan man had been ordered to ride over her—squash her flat if need be—to get the job done ... or else!

For hours this sensitive man had agonized over his employer's chilling directive, and the machine operator knew he could not do such a thing. He was not a sophisticated man, but he *was* a compassionate one. Unfortunately, reality is not so kind.

Mandegizi Umdaba, age thirty-seven, reached for the ignition key and turned off the monster earthmoving machine. On the grassy knoll adjacent to the burial site, the reconditioned 1970 diesel engine creaked like the door hinges of an ancient mausoleum and then sputtered to an eerie quiet. A creature of habit, Mandegizi locked the machine and dropped the key in his pants pocket. It did not occur to him that he need not worry about his mechanical equipment; only *he* and *the obstacle* were present. Mandegizi had not seen another person in these deserted woods since ... "No," his inner voice told him. "This is not the time to recall those sorry scenes." His subconscious swallowed the bad memories and gave him the go-ahead to jump down from the machine's platform.

Mandegizi made his way to the figure lying in the dirt. As he drew close, he reacted with shock. His mouth clamped shut like a startled clam. Nothing could have prepared him for this scene. As his fingers flew upward and pinched his nostrils shut, disbelief crossed his dark face. The odor of human waste was intense. So were his rampant thoughts: "Is this for real? She's naked as a jay bird and has obviously soiled herself. Who on planet Earth acts like this in this day and age?" In a blink of an eye, his disgusted attitude made an about-face, and pity grabbed his heart. With a sincere, compassionate tone of voice, he spoke: "Daughter of Africa, I beg you. My life will be as wretched as yours if I don't get my work done today. You *must* leave now. Please join your tribespeople ..."

Mandegizi released a long sigh. He didn't want to look like the big, bad wolf, but the woman left him no choice. "My orders are to ride over you. Is this what you want, to be a crushed daughter of Africa? In God's name, why would you wish to sacrifice your life for a piece of land? Are you crazy?"

The verbal assault hit Vimbela's heart like a rock and knocked the breath out of her. Rage bubbled up inside her. She rolled over, sat upright, and speechlessly stared Mandegizi down, surveying him. Although her clear vision was long gone, her glare settled on the unfamiliar face of a young, lanky man wearing a brown uniform that had a logo etched on the shirt pocket. His skin tone was blacker than hers. He had no facial hair, not even a five o'clock shadow. His short-styled hair was soft, not knotty like hers. He was not muscular, but somewhat wiry. And he definitely was not Zulu. His clumsy pronunciations were a dead giveaway.

Overpoweringly, Vimbela's mama-bear reared. She threw her head back, and a torrent of angry tears gushed out between her thinning, grey lashes. She put a finger to her lips in a silencing gesture: "Shhh. My ba-b-y is asleep," she stammered. "You musn't wa-ke my little child with your, um, dra-go-n's breath. This is um, a *s-a-cred* pla-a-ce, a very spir-ritual place." She paused to wipe off a blob of saliva that had drooled from her toothless mouth onto her double chin. Then, incredibly, anger mixed with desperation rerouted her speech impairment. She coherently roared, "You've no right to be here! You are *not* one of us! You're a traitor like my brother, Kumdi. He betrayed all of us, but he got what he deserved. Many summers ago he was shot in the head by an *umlungu*, a tall, ugly white man."

Vimbela balled her chubby fists. "Then there's another traitor, the wicked son of our noble witch doctor Twazli. His name was Sliman. He had darkness inside him that fooled us all. He was blindsided by the *umlungu* and their promises of riches. He's not buried here …"

"And look over there." She pointed to a circle of stones around a mound of earth. "That's Kelingo's grave. He was a driver who worked for an *umlungu* lawyer in the big city of Durban. Poor Kelingo. He was arrested and sent to prison for something he didn't do. Why he took the blame for the real killer of our chief, Anele, I don't know. But what I can tell you is that Kelingo died a broken man. His body was returned here by his children for burial on our sacred hill." She then began to mumble incoherently.

Mandegizi scratched his head, trying to remember something she had mentioned. A mental slap revitalized his effort. "Of course," he muttered under his breath. It had been headline news across Africa. He had read that Kelingo's arrest in 1998 for first-degree murder rested on a sole witness, the hearsay of a little boy whose name Mandegizi couldn't recall. Later, the boy's statement had been admissible in court: "I saw with my own eyes the old man Kelingo and the *umlungu* man, the one who comes in the big bird that falls from the sky."

This crime had been one of extraordinary professionalism, not committed by the hands of an amateur old man. Naturally, Kelingo had protested his innocence, but the court found the boy's statement credible. As a result, an innocent man had a date with the hangman. Eventually, forensic science finally exonerated Kelingo; it was proven that the boy had mistakenly identified Kelingo as being in the kraal on the night the women were shot. But it was too late for the old man who had been wrongly accused. A massive stroke ended Kelingo's life the day after his release.

The past events were not lost to Vimbela, either. She continued, "There is another man here who died of a broken heart; his name was Tekenya." This time she gestured to an unmarked grave. "The goat herder sleeps restlessly over there because he took his own life. He plunged a spear through his heart. And you want to know why?" she asked with her voice dipping immaturely. When she did not get an immediate response from the uniformed intruder, she simply resumed as if she were talking to the air. "You see, a very bad *umlungu* man, the one I mentioned earlier, took the love of Tekeyna's life, Anele, away from our village many, many summers ago …"

Vimbela's index finger directed Mandegizi to an area on a hill, a pile of stones and rock slabs built to resemble the shape of a person with arms outstretched. This spot marked Anele's resting place. There, draped on the rocky arms, lay wilted, circular burial garlands once woven with fresh, yellow, aromatic wildflowers similar to dandelions. They, along with their host, were as dead as doornails. "That's my adopted *umama's* sleeping place," Vimbela said. "She is whole now. The burial women made sure that the bullet hole in her head was healed."

Vimbela's eyes searched Mandegizi's. He was stone-faced, wearing a switched-off expression. He was becoming immune to Vimbela's long-winded monologue. But he couldn't help but notice the solitary tear sliding down her right cheek. "I have another baby," she said in a whisper. "Her name is Sh*ee*-I-ya," Vimbela pronounced phonetically. "In our language it means 'Forsaken One.' She's *umlungu*, you know. She was shot in the head, too, but *she* didn't die." Vimbela's voice became barely audible. "How do I know this?"

Mandegizi felt a familiar ring in his head upon hearing the name "Shiya." His concentration returned to Vimbela's ramblings.

"How do I know this?" she repeated. "Because Shiya, accompanied by her beautiful daughter, Brianna, attended *our* mother's funeral. Shiya wasn't scared of the sacred snake that came to guide Anele into the Invisible Kingdom of Souls, but Brianna was terrified."

With a million thoughts going through his head, the man from Nairobi could not think straight. And his rigid posture, stiff as a board, communicated his frustration. He reached in his shirt pocket and pulled out a small, square tin. If there was ever a time he needed a tranquilizing smoke, this was it.

Sitting on a broad tree stump, Mandegizi inhaled deeply on his hand-rolled cigarette. But the nicotine fix did not dissolve Vimbela's murderous, powerful, and compelling look. It remained as lethal as the goat herder's spear. In no mood for mental gymnastics, Mandegizi swivelled around and turned his back to Vimbela. But she was larger than life in his mind. As he puffed away, he had to admit that deep down he admired this crazy old woman. She was gutsy, fearless, and reminded him of his own mother, who was a no-nonsense woman. In Vimbela's shoes, she probably would have put up the same fight. His mom, however, did not have to endure this poor woman's suffering. No, his mother was safely and comfortably established in a modest home that he had bought for her in Nancefield, a township of Soweto, outside the city of Johannesburg.

After Mandegizi had relocated his family from Kenya earlier that year, he had signed on at the unemployment bureau in Johannesburg as an experienced machine operator. A few days later, he was hired by a white-owned construction company. This good luck enabled him to make his widowed mother's life even more tolerable. She had financial security and the love and support of a big family. But the courageous woman who was now before him was not as fortunate and, indeed, was homeless. He didn't want to reflect on Vimbela's circumstances at the moment. Instead, he had to consider something that would *not* fade away:

the imprinted directive from his boss.

When Mandegizi had arrived at the work yard that morning, he was approached by Mr. Pieter van Ouster, the construction company owner. His Afrikaans accent was thick. "Mandegizi, I need you to take care of a serious problem." Pieter exhaled noisily. "Near the flattened kraal site, there's an elderly woman known as the 'brainless one.' All weekend, she has been throwing stones at my workers on their lunch breaks. You were there, weren't you?"

Mandegizi's answer was misleading. "No, sir. I was assigned to the eastern area." Actually, he *had* bobbed and weaved out of the way of hurtling missiles thrown by a person hidden behind dense shrubbery.

"I contacted the local police," Pieter informed Mandegizi. "They told me they will only come out if a rock injures one of my employees, so I instructed one of my workmen to intimidate her, chase her away with a machete. It worked for a while, but now I hear she's back, playing sentinel over a bunch of old graves near the area mapped out for further park reserve extension." Pieter made eye contact with his stoical operator. "Mandegizi, if you value your employment and the extra money I give you to work weekends, you will deal with this. I don't care how. And keep it quiet. I don't want the press all over it. Get rid of her! Get rid of her!"

Pieter's clear-cut order had frozen Mandegizi's virtuous heart—and continued to do so to this very moment.

Now, his what-to-do-next thoughts were drowning him like fishing weights. So far, he had only scratched the surface of this problem. How he was going to solve it was another matter. He lit another cigarette and exhaled an enormous smoke ring, which hurtled toward Vimbela. She took no heed of the pollutant-packed halo as she absently let a handful of arid soil slip through her fingers. Appealing to Mandegizi's good side, she said, "Please don't do this. You see, my precious baby's remains (a malformed child who had been born in late 1945) rest beneath me." She took a huge gulp of air as if all her breath had left her body. She was going to get her words out, even if the struggle for contaminated oxygen suffocated her. "I will fight you with every breath in my body because I won't let you disturb the sleep of my baby or the eternal sleep of Chief Naboto Dingane or his wife Tuttia or her mother Umdanuna or the wise woman Granny Matudia or, especially, my *umama*, Anele."

Now that the air in her lungs was depleted, she had no choice but to inhale again sharply. The new intake sent her on a roll: "If you disturb Anele's eternal spirit, she will haunt you. She will call up the *Imikhuba*, Twazli, who is a powerful witch doctor. He will send the *little people* with big red eyes from the dark underworld. You won't like *them*. They are scary!"

Mandegizi shook his head and silently put in his two cents. "Without a doubt, this woman is two bricks short of a load, and she could talk the ears off a rabbit." At that very moment, he wanted to shake the life out of her—shut her up. Instead, he found himself apologizing aloud. "Look, I'm sorry about your home being demolished. I'm sorry about having to remove your dead, but ..."

Vimbela cut him short with a flip response: "Are you not my brother in color? Or has your blood turned *umlungu*?" She gave him the angry eye-roll. "The evil of the white man's blood must be in your veins!" she hissed as she cracked her knuckles. "Why else would you want to destroy a cemetery, a resting place of the dead? And yes, you have already taken the only home I've ever known. Isn't that enough land for the beasts to roam?"

The worker's head hung heavily on his chest. There was

an unspoken moment when they actually agreed on the same loathsome subject. Yes, he had played a role in her homelessness. And yes, his machine and other bulldozers had accomplished what they had set out to do—compact the land where once stood a living kraal, the home of the ancient Nguni people, Vimbela's tribe. The area was now lifeless, murdered by the new African government. Without hesitation, the newly appointed tourism minister, Xasa, had ordered the annexing of tribal properties so he could extend the boundaries of the Umfolozi game reserve. Tourism brought in big bucks—big, big bucks—and money was all that was needed to stay in power. Ka-ching!

Nothing remained that even hinted of the human life that had once flourished in this part of the bushland: not a proud hut; a flowering red bush used for tea; a cornfield; a vegetable garden (the pride and joy of the homesteaders); nor a makeshift barn that housed cattle, the tribes' precious livelihood. One day it had all been there. The next day, sure as hell, it was gone. And today their burial ground was about to meet the same fate—destruction for the creation of a new fence line.

The new government made promises to the tribe ... and then lied:

Their promise not to destroy Tswanas Kraal was a lie.

Their promise not to bring hardship or homelessness was a lie.

Their promise not to desecrate cemeteries was a lie.

Their talk about the escalating demand for safari tours—primarily to see Africa's elusive big five: lion, leopard, elephant, rhino, and buffalo—was the only thing that was not deceitful.

Mandegizi, a devout Catholic, understood that "money is the root of all evil," but to disobey orders ... He vigorously shook his head. No, he was not here to make sense of all this, and he was becoming more than tired of the moral dilemma. He had been up since well before dawn. He had travelled over forty miles in his old, beat-up truck to the workstation. If he did not put in his twelve-hour shift, he would not be paid, or worse, would be fired. He could not let that happen; there were millions of unemployed men who would jump into his shoes in a heartbeat. He felt a fierce pounding in his temples. The last thing he needed was to have his blood pressure out of control. Could he be a stabilizing influence? He doubted it, but he decided to make a last-minute attempt to prevail over this situation.

Mandegizi made eye contact with his belligerent antagonist. "Please understand that I'm only doing my job," he stated. "I have to feed my family. I have a widowed mother, an unemployed brother, two sisters, a wife, and three young children of my own whose mouths are always open." He extended his hand to help her rise. Vimbela looked at it as if it were covered in dung, and then her words came fast and furious. "I don't care if you have a hundred hungry children. You have taken my home. I'm not going to let you take *my* burial place. You're going to have to kill me first." She gave him a mocking, "I-dare-you" look, and turned away.

"I don't make the rules," Mandegizi huffed to her bare back. "And I don't work for the whites anymore," he added, tongue in cheek, as he quickly brushed away the pop-up image of Van Ouster's face. He added, "Not that it's going to cause you to change your foolhardy stubbornness. Don't you know that we have a black president?" He emphasized, "The new government is true *African*." Unleashing a long sigh, he felt he was being seduced into doing something he couldn't do—walk away. "A *black* ruling party," he stressed.

"It may not make a blind bit of difference to you, but this extra land is needed to house the many large animals white people from all over the world pay big money to see. The game park is going to be made bigger whether you and I like it or not! Now move, please, or you'll leave me no choice!" he ended harshly.

Civilized folk would have been intimidated by Mandegizi's tirade, but not Vimbela. Yes, her brain was shortchanged, but it did not stop her from knowing right from wrong. She was in the middle of a challenge she couldn't let slip away. She yelled at him, "This is our homeland, not the *umlungus'*. The white devils have no right to take from us what was ours to begin with."

At his wit's end, Mandegizi wrung his sweaty, sun-beaten hands. There was no meeting of the minds here. This was pure frustration, with absolutely no end in sight. And he was not here to rationalize the greedy economics, nor defend the government's ruling. Nevertheless, he could not begin to imagine what she was feeling or understand her primal background. He had been raised in a middle-class, working-family home. A question popped into his head: *Who is this tenacious woman?* So he asked, "Sister, what is your name? How old are you?"

"I'm called Vimbela, precious child of the Ancients, and I'm ageless ..." She broke her words to thump her fist on the ground. "I'm not your *sister*. My true brother, Kumdi, is dead. He was shot in the head years ago when the *umlungu* came and took my baby girl, Shiya. I gave her my milk. She was a white child, you know ..." Vimbela's body shuddered as her head flooded with bygone happenings.

Hadn't she played a big role in that remarkable scenario? In December of 1945 hadn't she been sent by the matriarch of the village, Granny Matudia, to fetch Chief Naboto from under the baobab (tribally named the "dead rat tree" because of its rodent-shaped, hairy fruit) to tell him that Anele was on her way home? Hadn't she breast-fed baby Shiya when Umia, another Tswanas nursing mother, refused? Hadn't she, a woman who was not the "sharpest tool in the shed," shared the raising of the child with Anele? Hadn't she hid in that same baobab tree with the five-year-old Shiya, when the tall, ugly, blonde *umlungu* man came to take her away?

Mandegizi wished he had never asked who she was. Without a shadow of doubt, she could keep talking until the cows come home.

Vimbela told him of the happy memory she had when Shiya, whom she had made strong with her milk, returned to Tswanas in mid-February 1998 for a visit, a short-lived reunion. Shiya, age fifty-three at the time, had been taken away by air ambulance. Soon after her departure, the Tswanas villagers buried their brutally assassinated chief, Anele.

Now all Vimbela could think about was a wish to have Shiya here standing next to her at the burial ground. *She* would have known what to do. She was rich, powerful, white, and wise to the ways of adults. But did she *invite* sorrows? Hell, no!

Mandegizi observed Vimbela's vacant, faraway look and shrugged. No, he did not want to blame this victim, but time was of the essence. So in a down-to-earth voice, he pleaded to the child within her. "Please, Vimbela, precious little daughter of the Ancients, I'm asking you to get up so I can go about my work. I will radio for help, for someone to come get you and take you to Soweto, where the rest of your tribe members are living. They've fancy new homes, nothing like what you are used to out here in the bush. There's good drinking water straight from a tap and lots of food at the shops. Sister Bertha, who helped relocate your people, will take good care of you."

Vimbela made an angry face. She didn't want to hear that name. In her simple mind, the nun was a sham. She had preached

about miracles and given false hope not only to Vimbela but to her
tribespeople, as well. Vimbela recalled the nun kneeling in prayer
and, afterward, reassuring them that her God *would* intervene—
turn back the excavators—and thus, save the village and burial
ground from destruction. It was all nonsense. And now Vimbela
had come to the end of her rope. She had tried her best to convince
Mandegizi not to destroy all that was holy to her, but she had
failed. There was only one thing left to convey ... loudly: "Only
over my cold, dead body! Do what you will!"

Mandegizi's steely grimace said it all. He had come to the end
of *his* rope. With Vimbela's unsettling, demonic cackle ringing in
his ears, he kicked up a storm behind him on his way back to the
excavator. Yes, it was unfair, unreasonable, and not right, and of
course, he did not want unclean hands, but what were the bleak
alternatives? He could join the tens of millions of unemployed,
become a homeless black person, or worse, starve to death.
The situation boiled down to this: him or her? Out of the blue,
a gruesome thought struck his good heart: "No one would bat
an eyelid if she simply vanished." His boss had made that point
clear. But Mandegizi was still torn. Thinking ahead, his insides
unequivocally declared, "Absolutely, no way. I can't do it! I just
can't!" In a flash, his shaky inner voice reminded him: "But your
neck is on the line."

Standing alongside his machine and rubbing his goosebumps
nervously, Mandegizi wanted to run away, just disappear. "It's
not supposed to be this way," his inner voice chimed.

Oh, how he hated this job.

Unbeknown to the machine operator, the worst scenario had
not yet reared its ugly head. There would be *dark* days ahead.

CHAPTER TWO

Nancefield, Soweto, the next day, Tuesday, December15, 2009

"Even God cannot change the past."
—AGATHON, 446-401 BC

MILES AWAY, and the day after Mandegizi fired up his bulldozer, a barefoot six-year-old African girl named Amalonda stepped over the frail body of her grandmother, who was curled up like a dog on the bare floor of a chilly hallway. The young girl walked out of her shabby, overcrowded home on Khoali Street in Nancefield Township. Her matchbox dwelling was built of corrugated iron sheets that housed herself; her maternal grandmother; and four of her older, idle, male relatives. Amalonda assumed her cousins were already out roaming the streets—getting into goodness knows what—because they couldn't find work in a country whose economy had shed millions of jobs since 1993.

Weighed down with responsibilities, Amalonda, the only child of Ithunzi Junior, Umia's deceased son, was an "old soul" who had been catapulted into maturity by circumstance. This little girl would never have the chance to be a carefree child because she was the primary caregiver to her sickly grandmother. It was Amalonda who cashed her grandmother's monthly pension check, a pittance of forty-two dollars. It was Amalonda who then purchased the costly antiviral medication that was her grandmother Umia's life support. When the money ran out, Amalonda scrounged for enough clean water, food, and medicine to keep them all alive. It was Amalonda who begged food from neighbors and strangers when there was nothing left in the larder.

On this bright Tuesday morning, in the front yard under the first rays of sunlight, Amalonda placed her hands on her stomach and pressed hard. But the pangs of hunger continued to grumble like the onset of a bad storm, just as they had all weekend. Food— there was never enough of it. Food was what she thought about day and night. But maybe today, with luck, her teacher would have a delight of some kind for her. It wasn't unusual for the kind-hearted, soft-spoken Sister Bertha to have fruit, a biscuit, or a tasty lollipop to hand out. Candy! What a magic word. Amalonda wanted to use her natural flexibility to express her happiness through cartwheels—but the unbearable pain of hunger held her back. So the spirited child ambled down the road, breaking up dusty dirt devils underfoot. She soon joined other children who were wearing matching uniforms and plodding their way down the pitted, garbage-strewn side road that led them to the schoolhouse, a trek of a mile and a half.

Behind her, in the part of the township Amalonda called home (a place that had been at the heart of the freedom struggle), coal-fired smoke belched from holes in the many tin roofs that housed impoverished people. Since she knew no other life, she accepted her lot in the ninety-square-mile settlement that had been set aside for blacks by the South African government in 1931. After the founding of Soweto (which was situated in the

bowl of municipal sewerage, land that the whites did not want),
no black person was permitted to live in the white-inhabited city
of Johannesburg. Three million people were forcibly resettled into
this black homeland. This designated lower-class area was nothing
more than a concentration camp, yet Soweto (South Western
Townships), Amalonda's birthplace, was an area of stark contrasts:
rows and rows of tin shanties abutted well-constructed, middle-
class brick homes that had indoor plumbing, electricity, modern
kitchen appliances, and up-to-date electronics.

From somewhere down the road, gramophone music blared.
Ella Fitzgerald's "Cry Me a River" assaulted Amalonda's ears; the
record obviously had seen better days. However, this happy-go-
lucky granddaughter of Umia, a Tswanas tribeswoman, didn't
give a hoot about the dreadful, distorted music or the racket of a
diesel train in the background. Her happy heart manifested itself
in a big smile as she anticipated receiving a snack at school.

Of course Amalonda knew nothing of the widening gap
between the rich and the poor that was fueling bitter class tensions
in South Africa, or of the racial ugliness of previous years. She did
not know that the resentment had grown so great in April 1976
that the Soweto schools went on strike and incited an "uprising"
of student-led protestors who fought the law that said that only
Afrikaans and English languages could be taught in Sowetan
schools. She did not know that during this ghastly struggle so
many people, mostly children, were killed by the South African
police. Of course, she had never heard of Hector Pieterson, who
was shot dead by police during the uprising. His death, the deaths
of numerous other victims of this bloodbath, and the June 1992
Inkatha Freedom Party massacre at Boipatong changed the course
of history.

Even if this awful period of racial hatred had been known

to Amalonda, it would not have made a dent in her intention to get to the Holy Cross primary school and enjoy a yummy bite of whatever was offered by her favorite teacher.

Awaiting the school children was a slender, stooped nun of medium height. Her poor posture hid the fact that she was only in her thirties. But there was no mistaking Sister Bertha's sparkle of youthfulness, charismatic intensity, and warm smile. Her onyx eyes and purplish complexion shone under the overhead neon lighting. She walked up and down the twenty-by-twenty-foot classroom placing the day's assignment, English spelling, onto turn-of-the-century, old-fashioned, hinged school desks that were complete with inkwells. She then put her hand into the pocket of her baggy, black, serge habit and retrieved stubs that were once full pencils. With the writing tools clasped in her hands, Bertha let out a resigned sigh. She had lost track of her many denied requests for additional money to buy basic school necessities, so even asking for money to buy a computer that could bring the Holy Cross school into the electronic era was out of the question. The Catholic Finance Committee, the official aid agency in Johannesburg, had this to say:

"Dear Sister Bertha,

"I am sorry to inform you that your request has been denied. The escalating costs of antiviral medicine to contain the AIDS epidemic must hold first place on the church's monetary agenda ... blah ... blah ... blah ..."

Naturally, Sister Bertha understood this priority. And yes, she had read in Catholic literature that the church budget was now at its lowest due to assistance given to impoverished victims. The wrath of the contagion was felt on every street in this nation, where it infected one in nine persons. And tragically, most of the children who attended this school were HIV positive.

"Without hope, there is no life for these poor souls," Bertha uttered under her breath.

She and her novice helper, Sister Claudia, age nineteen (a Soweto native), gave what they could from the school's scanty housekeeping budget to help others. But what else could they do? They were voluntary nuns. They had no monthly salary. And sometimes they themselves relied on donated food.

Of course Bertha had faith in God and prayed daily for a miracle. But it did cross her mind that He had turned His back on her for reasons that were unexplainable. It was a bitter pill to swallow: "Why haven't I burned my habit and thrown away my faith?" *He* had not protected her from the evil massacre that had befallen her village when she was a child—or from that *dark* day at a priest's residence.

Still, Bertha wasn't going to butt heads with her Maker. Not now.

She placed a hand on her high forehead and glanced at her watch. Children, ranging in age from five to ten years old, would soon be filling her classroom. It saddened her to think that many of her students' lives could be cut short at any time. But Bertha was resigned to make *this* day a happy and productive one.

As the extraordinary woman made her way to her heavy, colonial, oak desk, which was just as ancient as the rest of the school furniture, she grimaced. Agonizing muscle spasms seemed to be attacking every disc in her spine.

A few weeks ago, after many medical tests, Bertha learned from the convent's physician that she had an abnormal curvature of the spine. Her doctor suspected that untreated juvenile osteoporosis was the cause of her malady. Despite the fact that debilitating compression of her ribs on one side of her body was putting extreme pressure on her vital organs, Sister Bertha chose to get on with her life. She had refused further treatment. If the scoliosis was God's will, then so be it. She would suffer in His name. Had she not previously suffered worse than this disease? Bertha shrugged. She wasn't going to let the powers of reflection take her back to another time and place—her descent into the valley of death at the hands of a mortal man. "Yesterday is gone," she told herself. "Today is real."

In the few minutes she had before the arrival of the children, Bertha slumped heavily onto a chair and laid her veiled head on the wood surface of her desk. She shut her eyelids tight. Yes, she was sick. Yes, she had argued with higher authorities—no way was she going to retire and spend her days in cloistered solitude. And yes, she wanted to serve Christ by helping others until her last breath. Oh, she had come a long way from the life she once knew.

How had a little Muslim girl ended up becoming a bride of Christ?

CHAPTER THREE

Aweer tribal village near the coast of Kenya, thirty-five years earlier, 1974

IT WAS MARCH, the monsoon season.

In a heavily wooded forest near the border of Somalia, the sound of intense wailing blended with the sound of the heavy, midday rainfall bouncing off the severed tree branches that had been bent to form a basin in the earth. Inside this dugout she called home, Nthara, age thirteen, gave birth. It had been a long and hard delivery—over twenty-two hours of pushing, pushing, and more pushing—to bring her baby girl into the world. It should have been a joyous occasion, but this first-time mother's heart was anything but overjoyed. She had hoped for a boy because being born a girl was a curse. Girls were unwanted. Even in this modern age, girls were slaves, treated worse than livestock. Sometimes girls were forced to marry men forty years their senior. Conversely, sons were princes. They could do no wrong.

From a young age, males were taught that women were nothing

more than possessions. Men owned their women, and obey they must—or risk death, for the slightest disobedience. In the eyes of the menfolk, the female sex was unworthy, yet the girls and women were the backbone of this tribe. Women did the bulk of the work. They were the home builders. They gathered wood for cooking fires, collected water located half-an-hour's trek away, pounded millet, and climbed trees with the purpose of picking strange-looking wild fruits. The women fashioned clothing, kaftans and veils, from dyed black cloth. They stoked bonfires throughout the night to ward off predatory animals, especially during the calving season. But they did not provide meat. That task was up to the men and boys.

Nthara's people were not agriculturists, even though they kept a small herd of cattle for bartering at marketplaces. They were strictly hunters. More accurately, they were poachers, and at odds with the Kenyan law. The Aweer elders argued that their tribe lived off *their* land. Powerful longbows and poison-tipped arrows brought home meals of many different indigenous animals. Giraffes were a speciality. In addition, young, bare-chested sons used whistling signals to train fan-tailed ravens to locate honey, a staple food.

One survival tool this tribe lacked was education. It was forbidden. Also missing from the equation was music. Since time began, no instrument sounds or beautiful voices had ever been heard by this nomadic tribe. Music was forbidden.

Now, in the midst of a heavy downpour, the echoing cries from Nthara and her newborn reached the ears of the matriarch of the village. She entered Nthara's home and said, "You've birthed a boy, I hope."

Nthara's lowered head provoked the village elder's chilling reaction: "If you can't do it, I will."

"No, no," cried Nthara, as she protectively wrapped her arms around her newborn. "I can't smother my baby girl like many women have done. Please don't make me do it. I love my baby. I will keep her."

The elder made a face of disapproval before saying, "You know the rules. Your husband has the final say." With that said, the old woman left Nthara to her thoughts. Her husband, Sani, was not only her husband but also the all-powerful leader in the village. He was king. When a wife bore a son she was his queen. But when a wife bore a girl child, it was shame, rejection, and death to both mother and daughter, if the husband so chose. It was the husband's *right* to decide what to do with the baby girl. It was the husband's *right* to decide whether to get rid of Nthara and take another. The wife's only *right* was the naming of the girl child—if her husband let the newborn live. Naming of sons was strictly the father's privilege.

Nthara looked down at her healthy suckling baby and proclaimed her only right: "I name you Farida, sweet perfect girl."

Yes, baby Farida was perfect in every sense of the word. She wasn't bald like other village babies. Her baby had a full head of thick, black hair, and eyes adorned with long, silky eyelashes. Baby Farida's fingers and toes were slender, and her purplish skin glistened like the casing of a ripe plum. Her earlobes were large, believed to be a sign of beauty. But it was Farida's straight petite nose—not the typical African flat, broad-nose—that made this child stand out from the rest.

Young Nthara was more than proud. She made a vow to protect Farida with her own life. But there *was* one thing she could not prevent—the tribal custom that lay ahead for her child if she was allowed to live. The thought of it made Nthara shudder from head to toe. She, her mother before her, and her female relatives further back, had undergone the brutal mutilation of the coming-of-age circumcision ritual performed after first menstruation. This disturbing vision evaporated when Sani—wearing his best full-length, traditional Muslim *dishdasha* and *keffiyeh* turban held in place by a rope circlet—made his entrance. Smiling broadly at Nthara, he said, "*Inshallah*. You have given me a son?"

Nthara lowered her head as far as it would go, which was the custom. No woman could make eye contact with a man, even her husband. "No, husband," she replied shakily in Kiswahili. "Not this time. But *Inshallah*," she added respectfully, to please him. "God be with me. I will give you a son next time."

Sani's lips curled into a sneer that reached the tip of his nose. "Still more girls!" he raged. He quoted an Arabic text from the Koran and stormed out of the simple home like an enraged bull. The blood drained from Nthara's face as fear gripped her throat. Tears stung the back of her eyes as she shook from head to toe worrying about the unknown. She could do nothing but await her fate and that of her newborn.

Outside, in the tribe's gathering place—a circular ring of boulders placed around a water well—Sani, now a fifty-year-old deflated father, announced the sex of his latest offspring. Most of the men shook their heads. One old man commiserated by saying: "For sure a son will be born sooner or later to your young wife."

But Sani doubted. He was convinced that *his* God, Allah, was displeased with him because Nthara, his third wife, worshipped the mountain God, Ngai, behind his back. But then, Sani's other wives, who followed the teaching of Islam, had not given him a son either. Sani didn't know that the word "aweer," the ancestral name of his tribe, meant *unlucky*. Nor was he conscious of the fact that he was, without a doubt, *lucky* to have wives at all, given the fact that a few generations ago the slave trade had run rampant along this coast. The strongest men and boys and most of the village women and pubescent girls were yoked, chained, and marched to waiting slave ships moored on the east coast. Males now outnumbered females.

Nthara, unlike her husband, was illiterate, as was most of the tribe. But her mind was not ignorant. She knew that Ngai was the *only* God. However, she was often forced to listen to her husband ramble on about the strict teachings of Islam concerning women: Obedience to man and his law. Women should be submissive and obey their husbands—without question. Oh, she had tried, but today his cold-hearted disregard for their firstborn was more than Nthara could bear. She wept until her tears turned to anger. "My child will be different from all the rest of the Aweer children," she proclaimed. "She will stamp on the traditions of men. *She* will become our leader." Eventually, her outspoken lament would help her to deal with her broken heart.

As the years passed, little Farida, now age seven, was a dutiful daughter. She woke up daily at sunrise. She beat the cowhides used as mattresses, swept the living quarters, fed the camels, took the cows to pasture hours away, and then led them home at sunset, while carrying a sack of dried dung to be used as fire starters. It was hard work for a small girl, but she never questioned the many tasks assigned to her by her mother, who was in the last trimester of her sixth pregnancy. No, Nthara's firstborn child never complained.

When Farida wasn't confined to daily chores or looking after her younger siblings (all girls, ranging from a curious toddler to rambunctious five-year-old twins), she sneaked out of the village for "time out." These moments were rare, but when an opportunity rose, she took off like a rabbit into the wilderness—without first asking permission.

Farida ran into the savannah. The grass was tall, and it got taller as she moved farther into it. She loved to lie in the grass and gaze up at the stars. If she were caught, she could be beaten by her father. She had a problem with her father's authority in her life — especially with his *right* to choose a marriage partner for her. In her culture it was not unusual for girls to be married off at ten years of age. And Farida had no concept of time or her age. Nor did she have any real comprehension of religion. All she knew was that the sun marked the beginning and end of the day.

Gazing up at the stars, a not-so-glittery scene crossed her mind. Was she nearing the customary bridal age? It was not something she wished to think because she wasn't brainwashed — as were the other little girls — into thinking that an arranged marriage, having sons, and housekeeping chores would be a wonderful future. She didn't care if she was "left on the shelf" to become a mocked and shunned old maid. Besides, she didn't like boys. They were rowdy and rude. However, unbeknown to her, her sultry, Cleopatra looks had not gone unnoticed. There wasn't an eligible boy or old man in the village who didn't have his eye on her. Even the married men, young and old, thought she would make a suitable addition to a full house. It did not take long for Farida's outlook regarding marital customs to be challenged.

One night after all her chores were carried out, Farida's father forced her to parade in front of the men who, according to the Muslim faith, can marry a child. And consummating the marriage at seven years was acceptable. The world wasn't going to wake up too soon to this deplorable, pedophiliac Muslim practice or to the fact that "modern" slavery was the norm in this tribal village.

Sani announced, "She's a beauty, isn't she? Allah be praised. She will make a fine virgin wife. I will get a good return if I take her to the marketplace, don't you think? But you all know that it is the custom of our village to first present her to the men of the village. Who is going to make me an offer I can't refuse?"

Old men drooled, young men smiled, and boys grinned. They would have to work hard for years before they could offer enough cattle (gold was unheard of in this village) for *this* bride.

As soon as her father released his tight grip on her hand, Farida fled back to the dugout, buried her face into a fleece rug, and wept.

Shortly after the offer that had made Farida's cheeks glow like hot coals, an eleven-year-old slave girl from Berhano, a remote tribal village southwest of Mogadishu, Somalia, her feet bound with rope, was brought into the village. She became the focus of Sani's ardent attention. His lust was obvious. Farida could not have known that this tall, simple girl, amply endowed for her age, was nothing more than a sexual object among the men of Berhano. Handing her over to an Aweer elder in exchange for cattle was effortless for them. The headman of the girl's village had sought out the Aweer tribe. His people were suffering from a severe drought that had wiped out most of the village livestock. The young sex-slave was payment for cattle.

Mafua, the girl from Berhano, became Sani's fourth wife and later gave him the son he always wanted. Sani was so smitten with his new wife that he never again slept with his other wives, the mothers of his ten daughters. Some said Mafua was the spell-breaker who ended Sani's curse of siring only girls. Others said Allah had sent Mafua to heal the son-less man's devastated heart. Yes, the slave girl had indeed ended the baby-girl jinx, but she was hated by the other wives, who were now mocked and left to fend for themselves, according to custom.

Even so, Sani still had the *right* to marry off his daughters, and they were brought up in the fundamental teachings of the Islamic faith. They had to wear veils and long-sleeved clothing, attend prayers five times a day, and be obedient and submissive to men, or they would be beaten. Females could not eat before the men had their fill, and they could not talk to men unless spoken to. Once married, their husbands had the *right* to beat them. And wives could not return to their family home for any reason. Only Nthara was allowed to remain in the home she once shared with Sani.

A Muslim man is permitted to have four wives and a temporary wife (prostitute) for an hour at his discretion, yet ex-wives who are ousted from the marital bed are forbidden to take another man. So the now twenty-year-old Nthara carried a heavy sadness, as if she were walking with weights in her pockets. She was often lonely for male companionship, someone to cuddle with at night. And now she had little choice but to walk with her head down when an eligible male approached. Even looking at another man, for any reason, would have resulted in death by stoning. But if she fled the village, where would she go? Other tribes had their own culture, language, customs, and myths of origin. She would not fit in and probably never would be accepted. Or worse, she, like Mafua, could be sold to another nomadic tribe. Horrible stories came back about women who had been ousted from their tribes.

Nthara, her mind made up, was not going to risk a stolen embrace that could result in never seeing her children again. The thought of never seeing her favorite child, Farida, stopped short all possible dreams of flight. There was something special about her firstborn, but Nthara could not put her finger on it. If she could have glimpsed into the future, she would have seen just how *special* Farida was. One day the God, Ngai, would see fit to reward loyal Nthara's devotedness.

For the moment, spirited little Farida was doing what she loved to do—sneak out of the village before darkness fell. She headed for the open grassland to experience an "aha" moment: watching ostriches during their mating season. She lay on her stomach and marvelled at the long necks and legs of the males, and at the bright pink color they turned to attract females. Little Farida loved these creatures and had often been upset at having to partake of their flesh. When an ousted wife was able to snare one, the birds provided lots of meat for the dinner table.

On this particular evening, a warm breeze blew across the grassland in this tropical region. A female ostrich donning dull brown feathers twisted her long neck and looked straight at the child, who was trying to hide inconspicuously in the tall grass. Farida was more afraid of the big bird than she cared to admit. Hadn't she seen the scars on women who had been soccer-kicked by these mighty birds? "Shoo," Farida said in a voice that revealed a trace of fear. When the ostrich paid no heed, Farida got up and stamped her feet. The spooked bird sprinted in one direction, and Farida sprinted in the other. Later that night, Farida told the tale of the ostrich to her siblings. She described how she nearly got kicked by a giant bird but had scared it away. Farida loved to tell enthralling stories. But it was her infectious laughter that brought smiles to most faces.

During her childhood in the village of her birth, Farida was content, until, at age seven, the real *darkness* descended upon her happy-go-lucky demeanor. The aftermath of this gloom would eclipse her heart and soul forever. It never dawned on her that the secret the older girls kept from her was about to manifest itself.

At sunrise Farida awoke to menstrual blood pooling on the cowhide. "I'm too young for womanhood," she cried and then yelled for her mother. "Mother, I have the monthly blood of a woman. How can this be? I'm still a child."

Nthara was not surprised. She had been of the same age when the monthly cycle appeared. She bent down and placed her arms around her wide-eyed daughter. "God has smiled on you. You are a woman now. Sani will find you a husband." That was the last thing Farida wanted to hear, but protesting the subject was fruitless.

Nthara showed her daughter how to line her underwear with vine leaves and brewed her a tea made from the same plant. "Drink this," Nthara said. "It will help the cramping."

A few days before Farida's next blood flow, Nthara announced, "Come, Farida. It is time." Her command was lost on Farida, but not her mother's appearance. "You have your best wrap and veil on! Where are we going, Mother?"

No answer could have explained what was in store for young Farida.

Farida was taken to a clearing at the far end of the village, where the darkest evil descended. The older women held her down to prevent her from moving. The unsterile shard of glass that was held in the hand of the matriarch of the village glinted like a razor-sharp gladiator's sword in the sunlight. Farida, her eyes wide, her body bare from the waist down, her genitalia exposed for all to see, felt her heart race wildly, as if it were about to pop out of her chest. Her eyes darted to her mother. Farida thought, "*She can make this nightmare end.*"

How innocent—and wrong—she was!

Nthara, eyes rolled upward, stood silent as her daughter's eyes filled with hot, panicked tears. Farida knew from the helpless expression on her mother's face that she wasn't going to intervene. But Farida still tried to reach out to the woman who had given her life. "Mother, Mother, help me!" she sobbed. "The old lady is going to cut me up for a stew ..."

The most searing pain she had ever felt stopped her words and gave rise to the loudest scream she had ever emitted. Her ear-splitting wails continued to pierce the humid air, just like the sharp object that had removed her clitoris. Mercifully, she passed out. She did not hear the festive jumping to the beat ... nor could she recall the sounds of the similar congratulatory goings-on that had previously occurred—without an honest explanation.

When she finally came to, Farida could barely move. Her upper jaw, with its missing teeth, clamped on to her bottom lip. She felt like she had been shredded apart. The traumatized girl, her eyes darting from side to side, was so riddled with shock that she didn't utter a sound. Her genitalia were crudely stitched, and her legs were bound with strips of cloth. This brutal introduction into womanhood had a profound, silencing effect on her. She had not known what humiliation was until this moment. Diabolical degradation—such as this life-shattering experience—has a way of stalking the innocent. What she didn't know was that another diabolical event of a similar nature would revisit her, without mercy, in the future.

That night, the full moon rose into the heavens accompanied by a hellish red glow. Farida was breathing heavily as she crouched in the grassy plain. Hidden in the savannah, she looked up at the sky and prayed for the March seasonal rain to fall. She needed the steady downpour to weep with her and wash away the pain from her body and heart. It was a tall order for a deeply wounded young girl.

Farida's hands fiercely clutched her abdomen. She began to shake, not from the pain ripping through her body but from a dreadful feeling in her gut that something terrible was about to happen. But could anything be worse than what had already befallen her?

She did not know that the ethnic pot of simmering discord would soon come to a boil on a dark, red, vapor-streaked night like this. Nor did she know that the venomous threat of tribalism clashing over land was real. The impending mob scene, fortified by personal vengeance, would alter her Aweer roots forever.

For the duration of the forty-day genital binding, the once cheerful Farida turned sullen and temperamental, and became unwilling to help. Even her passion for storytelling vanished. She no longer beamed with a glorious smile. Nor did she whistle happy tunes when she was out of earshot. Her infectious laughter had also died. All she could think about now was running a spear through the heart of the old woman who had mutilated her.

Many years later, when Farida became Sister Bertha, she would come to understand that there was no guilt or punishment for ancient tribal ways. The Aweer were creatures of habit. Nothing could change their primitive way of life. Their customs had continued for centuries and would continue to do so in a *cursed* universe. They knew no better.

Before her bandaging was to be removed, Farida, with an eternal broken heart, fell asleep before nightfall in the comfort of the grassland, her security blanket. Suddenly, she was jerked awake by a bombardment of intense shouting, screaming, and crying that seemed to be rushing toward her from all directions. What was happening? She stood up and frowned. Why were the bonfires higher than normal? She put a hand across her nose. What was the disgusting smell wafting toward her? She untied her leg restraints to move faster.

Farida entered the village perimeter. There, in front of her, were strange dark men setting every home on fire with blazing torches. The mob scene was moving toward personal vengeance—an ethic pot of neighboring tribesmen clashing over land. She clamped her mouth shut as she watched in horror the stabbing deaths of men, women, and children who were fleeing from their burning homes. Destroy the women and you destroy the village.

With her jaw set, the gravity of the discovery hit home. Farida's first instinct was to run to her mother's place at the end of the village. But she sensed that even if she managed to escape the fire torches, she would be killed, for sure. Her heart was pounding against her skinny ribcage, and she became so terrified she wet herself. She swallowed a cry as the urine stung her mutilated genitals. She felt that she too was burning, though in a different way. She removed her veil and fashioned a diaper of sorts. This indignity was the least of her concerns. What could she do? She was a child. How could she, alone, stop this bloodshed and fight off these intruders?

With fear pervading her body, heart, and soul, Farida ran away as fast as she could through the grassland and into the forest. There, she climbed the tallest broad-leaved tree. She was lost ... scared ... hurt.

Hidden under a dense foliage canopy, her emotions burned angrily. She vowed, "I won't let my life end now. I won't let Death swallow me up like the mouth of a lion." Silently she prayed: "Allah, the merciful, save me. And save my mother and sisters and friends ..." She gasped fearfully. The solitary roar of a lion was deafening, as was the sound of thunder. Suddenly, the dark, rain-laden sky began to weep, showering the pitiful child, whose eyes were puffy from tears. Farida was clinging desperately to a tree. For hours she was afraid to close her eyes, but exhaustion was tugging at her enforced wakefulness. Her eyelids drooped ... snapped open ... drooped ... snapped open. It didn't take long for her drooping eyelids to triumph.

With her bare bottom wedged in a hollow and her legs straddling either side of the tree trunk, she was out for the count and didn't hear a thing.

Subconsciously floating through the Netherworld, Farida saw

her mother bathed in a blue light, with her arms outstretched.

"I'm coming, Mother. I'm coming," Farida cried.

The spoken voice was not of *this* world. "It's not time, child. You are an orphan of Destiny. Only *she* can lead you now."

CHAPTER FOUR

The Aweer village, the day after the tribal bloodbath

"OUR MERCIFUL GOD in Heaven has spared your life," a voice boomed upward.

The intense afternoon sun was cooking every living thing in the forest that surrounded the ravaged village. Native babul trees welcomed the fierce heat, but seedling evergreens—and the chubby man walking in the bush to relieve himself—did not. As a cone hurtled down toward the gentleman, he ducked. He looked upward expecting to find a monkey toying with him. Reverend Ochiagha could not believe his eyes. Was it a trick? Had the cruel sun affected him? Was a child up there? Who was she? And why had she been spared?

The Anglican minister was stunned that *someone* had actually survived the massacre. Earlier, he and his fellow missionaries had stumbled upon the carnage and buried all the dead in a communal grave.

"Climb down, child," the Reverend coaxed. "No one is going to hurt you."

Wrenched from one world into another, Farida trembled and, with knitted eyebrows, wondered, "Who is this bald, dark stranger standing underneath the tree wearing an ankle-length, brown garment with a white neck collar? What is he saying?" One thing she did understand was his beckoning climb-down gesture. Should she trust him?

As if reading her mind, Tomas Ochiagha soothed, "Child, I'm a man of God. He sent me to take you somewhere safe."

Still no wiser and deathly afraid, Farida was of two minds: A part of her knew she couldn't spend another uncomfortable moment in this tree. She was tired, hungry, and desperate for the touch of anyone who could take away the emptiness in her heart. Another part of her was terrified. Had this stranger accompanied the marauding tribesmen? Was he here to kill her?

Little Farida's parched tongue and dry throat overpowered her hesitation. She took several deep breaths and began to descend. Her legs were shaking so badly that she slipped several times, but she was always able to steady herself by wrapping her legs around a tree branch.

As soon as her bare feet were on solid ground, her savior, with his bathroom urge now on the backburner, reached into his tunic pocket and handed her a biscuit and a small bottle of fresh water, both of which she vigorously devoured. With her emotions flying in every direction, she fell to her knees and sobbed.

As Farida firmly interlaced her fingers, she was helped to the waiting Land Rover. She took one look at the strange contraption and let out a shriek that sent a flock of drongo birds soaring. Her feet were ready to follow the birds, but Ochiagha's arms instinctively reached out and encircled the naked, frightened child. "Don't be afraid," he comforted, as he covered her trembling body with a blanket handed to him by a fellow missionary. She looked so pitiful wrapped in a cover of rough hemp.

Clueless as to what the strange man had said, Farida fearfully began her uncharted journey curled up on the car's floorboard in the space behind the front passenger seat. Every gear shift, revving sound, honk, and bump sent her into wails. Unable to speak Kiswahili, Tomas reached behind the front seat and patted the girl's head in a soothing motion to allay her fears. But the more he patted, the more she shrieked. His driver, a fellow missionary who didn't speak her language either, spoke up, "It's obvious the poor child is petrified. She has never known the world beyond her village. When we reach our destination, I'm sure that we will find someone who understands her language."

In the dead of night, after a ten-and-a-half-hour drive, they reached "the place of cool waters"—Nairobi. Reverend Ochiagha was relieved. So was his driver. In order to keep the strong odor of the child's urine from overpowering their nostrils and spoiling their clothing, they had driven the entire way with the windows open … through a raging sandstorm. Every person in the vehicle was layered with fine sand particles.

It was agreed that their first stop would be a Red Cross Station … closed.

The second stop was Refugee International … also closed.

The third stop was a police station. The visit there was as fruitless as the search for the fountain of youth.

The fourth stop was a well-known orphanage. Although the head of the orphanage was genuinely sympathetic, her answer was, "We are full to the brim. We can't feed another soul."

Although they were almost out of options, there was one more stop. Was it worth a try? Ochiagha's driver didn't think so, but

Ochiagha wondered, "Why not?" It was now four o'clock in the morning, and he was exhausted.

An hour later, armed with a map drawn by the last "no-we-can't-help" orphanage person, they arrived at Mother of Mercy convent. The run-down building, constructed of brick with a slate roof, was home to elderly retired nuns who were dedicated to prayer in both silence and solitude. No child, teenager, or adult from the outside world had ever been permitted to enter. Today would be an exception.

The sleepy-eyed girl fiercely clutched the cleric's hand. Her knees were knocking as she climbed the stone stairway that led to the convent's heavy, paneled door. Confused, she had no idea what lay in store for her or why she had been brought to this strange place. However, she still tried to take in the sights and sounds of a world she had never dreamed existed.

In response to the holy man's determined knocking, a veiled face appeared through a small, double-grilled window. Farida took one look at the ghostly face, let out a scream, and then hastily cowered behind her escort.

In a weary voice the nun whispered, "Can I help you?"

"Sister, I'm sorry to intrude on your privacy ..."

The nun cut in. "Excuse me for interrupting, but our rising time is not until five-thirty. Come back then." Her eyes focused on the gentleman's stiff, white neck collar. "Are you a man of God?"

"Yes, Sister," he replied. "I'm an Anglican minister, ordained at St. Margaret's in Great Britain. I'm on a sabbatical, and I was travelling to Mount Kenya when ..."

"Who is the child?"

"Oh, it's a long and difficult story to explain, Sister," he sighed. "But *she* is the reason I need to speak to Mother Superior."

"I see," the nun uttered. "Wait there, please. I have to consult with the Mother Superior, and I'll be back shortly."

Soon the heavy door was opened by the same elderly nun who obviously had dressed in a hurry. Her headpiece was askew, her habit loose, and her belt of rosary beads missing. Farida and the Reverend were ushered into the vestibule. The nun's nose wrinkled involuntarily. "Good Heavens! She has soiled herself."

Ochiagha bowed his head. What could he say?

The nun ran off in a flash and returned with a group of nuns who were led by a stocky woman wearing thick-rimmed glasses. The lead nun stepped forward and addressed Ochiagha: "The work of this house is prayer in silence. We do not allow visitors here."

Farida's eyes darted first to the rotund woman, then, individually, to the others, and then around the sixteen-by-sixteen-foot lobby. Never had she seen so many corpulent black women gathered in one spot, all wearing unfamiliar clothing. Most of her village women were thin from malnourishment, and they never had time to cluster; they were too busy working. Farida's thoughts were distracted by the height of the ceiling, which appeared to be as tall as the sky. Wood-framed religious pictures hung on every available wall space, and vases containing an assortment of colorful tropical flowers adorned hallway tables. The tiled floor shone with polish that reflected her image ... and displayed the bright yellow color of urine.

A holy woman rushed over and, with sash pulleys, slid open a large single-pane window.

Ochiagha, his dark cheeks reddening with embarrassment, apologized. "I'm so sorry, Sisters, but I had nowhere else to take this poor, unfortunate child, and yes, she has soiled herself. At this hour I was unable to find washing facilities to clean her. This girl is of the Aweer tribe. I'm sure word has not reached you yet, but she's the only survivor we could find after the mass execution of her tribespeople. Unfortunately, most refuge institutions and orphanages are chock-o-block full, so I brought her here until I can find alternative housing. Is that all right with you, Mother Superior?"

The nun sighed sympathetically. She could unequivocally relate to this tiny victim. No one could possibly imagine the carnage unless they had been through it—and she had. At a similar age to this child's, an intensive killing campaign by rival factions in *her* Ethiopian village had robbed Clara of her father, mother, grandparents, aunts, uncles, and ten siblings. Every female, young and old, in her village had been raped, had their throats slit, and been left to bleed to death. Miraculously, like Farida, she alone had survived and lived in a deplorable refugee camp for five years before begging the nuns to let her enter this convent. That was almost fifty-five years ago.

Now, Clara, her eyes heavenward, silently said, "Thank you, Jesus. You were watching over me when the knife failed to sever my artery that horrible day all those many years ago." Clara then turned to the group of nuns standing behind her, curiosity lining their faces, and asked, "Do any of you speak Kiswahili?"

A chubby nun answered softly. "I do, Mother Superior. I was born not far from her village." Before Clara could speak further on the matter, Reverend Ochiagha piped up. "Good. Tell her she is safe here and in God's merciful hands."

In the time that followed Farida's entry into the convent, she saw her dreams and her life as she had known it slip away. The loss of her parents, siblings, friends, and village life were an entrenched emptiness in her heart. She was an orphan. There was no one to claim her. What were her chances of surviving outside the confines of this strict Carmelite order? Although her new benefactors were kind to her, she was soon forced to think like an adult, act like an adult, and endure baptism into a religion that was foreign to her. At age twelve (an age given to her because there was no accurate birth date), she had no "calling" to serve the Christian God. Her father's strict Islamic teachings remained imprinted.

But as the sands of time passed, chastity, poverty, and obedience became natural to her. Her typical day at the convent started at 5:30 A.M—rising time. The day, spent mostly in prayer, ended at 10:30 P.M.—lights out.

At age sixteen, Farida became a novice.

At age eighteen, she took permanent vows.

Thus, Sister Bertha was born. Little Muslim Farida became history.

CHAPTER FIVE

Carmelite Convent, Nairobi, the start of the New Year 1996

HAVING STUDIED RESOLUTELY, Sister Bertha, now twenty-two years old, finally received her bachelor's degree in teaching, a noble profession she thought would be spiritually rewarding. But her strong desire to leave the convent and educate bush children was not well met. "We have nuns here who are illiterate," Mother Superior, the eighty-year-old head of the convent, informed Bertha. "Your training is much needed right here."

Forbidden to speak aloud, Bertha hurriedly scribbled her response in a notebook she carried with her at all times. "With due respect, Mother Superior," she wrote, "there are so many poor children who need ..."

Clara intercepted in a whisper. "There are no 'buts' about it. You will put your training, paid for by this convent, to good use here." She thrust the notebook back into Bertha's hand. "I don't want to hear another word about it. No more talk about this,"

Clara said. "Off you go to prayers," she ended sternly.

Bertha's sandals, made of tire rubber, thumped down the corridor toward the chapel. Although she had been put down, a not-so-dutiful Farida was resurrecting herself with every step. She felt like an emotional prisoner who was locked from the inside.

A year later, January 3, 1997, Mother Superior yielded to the constant barrage of Bertha's request notes. "I was wrong about you, Sister Bertha," Clara admitted. "You are truly gifted. There isn't a Sister under this roof who hasn't benefitted from your educational knowledge. So you have my blessing to go out in the world and put the gift Christ has given you to good use."

Bertha's broad smile said it all.

The next morning, as Sister Bertha left to pursue her greatest dream—educating those who otherwise would not be able to receive the gift of knowledge—she was given bus fare, a supply of food, extra clothing, and of course, well wishes from Clara. Bertha put all the handwritten goodbye notes from her fellow nuns in her notebook. She would treasure them.

Prior to her departure, the twenty-three-year-old nun had read in the newspapers that a lot of schools across Africa were in dire need of English teachers. A posting caught her eye: "English teacher wanted immediately for Catholic elementary school in Pongola, Zululand."

All it took was a "forbidden" telephone call to the school's principal, and Bertha was accepted without hesitation. The eager school official had one burning question: "When can you start, Sister?"

"I'm planning to leave the convent tomorrow."

Bertha instantly settled into her new life outside the convent walls, with gusto. The Pongola school children were a delight. Her sparsely-furnished one-bedroom apartment above the school was a delight. But being able to speak without permission and eat when she wanted to were the best delights of all. Bertha couldn't have been happier. But one day her new life abruptly changed.

It was a Saturday morning, two weeks after her arrival at the school. Bertha decided to go to the local market town and check out its wares. While there, she met the frail, elderly Anele Dingane and her daughter, Insikazi, who were from Tswanas Kraal, a remote settlement south of Pongola.

On Saturdays at the crack of dawn, the women carried baskets, exited the kraal, and walked a mile over a long, narrow hilltop to catch a bus to the market town. The charming Tswanas women set up their shop to sell beaded jewelry encased with various semiprecious stones, along with a variety of garden produce.

On this fine start of a summer weekend, Insikazi spotted Bertha at an adjacent stall. It was the first time she had seen a nun in full attire, and she was intrigued. Insikazi couldn't help but notice Bertha's sultry Cleopatra looks, but it was the glorious smile Bertha gave to the vendor she was talking with that captivated Insikazi the most. She hoped the nun would come over to her stall. She was eager to talk to the woman who was standing out like a sore thumb.

The sparkling items of jewelry displayed on the Tswanas table caught Bertha's eye.

"Good morning, ladies," she greeted as picked up a bead bracelet encased with amethyst chips. "Oh, this is so pretty. Did you make this?"

"All this jewelry is made by our tribespeople in Tswanas," Insikazi responded. Instead of using her usual selling tactics to encourage Bertha to buy the piece, Insikazi remarked, "If you don't mind me saying so, you are a beautiful woman and obviously not from these parts. What brings you here to Pongola?"

Sister Bertha smiled. Flattery was new to her. However, she was not prepared for the personal, rapid-fire questions from Anele, who rose from her chair to make eye-contact. "Couldn't you find a good husband? Is that why you chose to become a nun? Men in my village would give their eye-teeth for a good-looking woman like you."

Though not shocked, Bertha was surprised by Anele's fluent, refined English accent. Had she been in the whites' service? If not, what school had she attended? Bertha could see that Anele was in poor health, but this charming woman had a magnetic, youthful personality. It was Bertha who was now intrigued. "Where did you learn to speak English so well?"

Anele did not explain her fluency. Instead, she repeated her daughter's question: "Do you live in Pongola, and what are you doing here?"

"Yes. I have a teaching job."

Anele's eyes, clouded with the onset of cataracts, lit up as she sprang into action. "How would you like to come to Tswanas and teach our children? It has been many long years since our teacher, who was also a nun, died horribly. We have never been able to find a replacement for this great woman. I can pay you well."

Bertha found herself torn by the offer and the mention of "dying horribly." What did Anele mean by that? She didn't dwell long on the subject because in her heart of hearts, she wanted to accept the proposed good paying teacher's job. But money wasn't everything. The image of the children she had been teaching without pay for two weeks made her decline the offer. It was unthinkable to give up on these kids.

"I'm grateful for your offer, but I'm already employed," Bertha said with a warm smile.

Anele was not smiling. She was not a defeatist, and she set out to change Bertha's mind. "Please reconsider, Sister. Our children are desperately in need of Christian guidance," she said glibly. Christianity was her snare, not her true intention. Basic education was her goal. Anele walked around to the front of the stall and clasped Bertha's hand. "Many years back, we were lucky to have Sister Babavana, who, I believe, was from your part of the world. But we didn't have her for long. During a school break, she returned to her Aweer village to see her family. She was murdered in a tribal uprising that same day ..."

Bertha's gasp ended Anele's words, but not her own, "Did you say *Aweer*?"

Anele nodded.

Motionless, Bertha found herself drifting back into a sea of memory. The windows to the past opened. She wondered if *they* could have been related. Had this woman, Babavana, also been a little girl handed over to a convent? Even though this fact was unknown, the thought of walking in the footsteps of a possible deceased relative clinched the deal.

"I've changed my mind," Bertha said. "I would love to teach your children, but first I have to give my notice. Then I will have to get permission from Mother Superior."

Permission was received.

Two months later, April 1997, living and working in the isolated Tswanas village in Zululand was by far the happiest life Sister Bertha had ever known. Fetching water from the nearby river, washing laundry on the banks, and collecting firewood for a communal cookout all took her back to her childhood ... that is, before her genital mutilation in the Aweer settlement. What really made Bertha content was that the barbaric practice did not exist in Zululand.

Bertha turned a diplomatic blind eye to the other pagan rituals that were carried out by the young Tswanas witch doctor, Sliman. However, she avoided him, even though every woman in the kraal swooned when he walked by. The witch doctor was superficially charming, and his jet-black eyes sparkled flirtatiously when he spoke. He was always dressed immaculately, which surprised Bertha. How could it be that his cotton pants and crisp shirts did not sport even one wrinkle? Certainly, there were no pressing irons here. It did not take Bertha long to learn that a besotted woman in the village placed hot, flat rocks on his wet, folded outfits for hours before she hung them on the laundry line using the wooden pegs that Anele had fashioned from twigs long ago. Voilà!

After a little persuasion, Bertha's religious attire received the same consideration.

Although her heavy garb was cumbersome and unbearably hot at times, Bertha was resigned. Modesty was one of the holy vows she had taken. It wasn't until a little girl laughingly said, "You are going to cook like the meat in the stew pot if you don't take off your silly clothing," that Bertha decided to wear lighter fabric full-length dress and a cotton headscarf over her shaven head. The only time her habit and starched black-and-white headdress would be donned was when she was summoned back to the convent. The thought of her previous visit to the convent to obtain permission to work in a "pagan" kraal made her cheeks blush with guilt. And it wasn't the reunion with her fellow sisters that made her heart race—it was a priest. She was first aware of an attraction—her first puppy love crush—while at the convent shortly before getting her teaching degree. Samuel's glorious smile and perfect teeth left her feeling giddy. And she was deeply captivated by his deep tenor voice. It sent tremors down her spine.

But all was not what it seemed.

Father Samuel Ungobo, age twenty-eight, was Ugandan-born

and had entered the priesthood in his teens. Samuel replaced the old, sickly priest who had administered last rites to dying nuns for too many years to count. A fresh, young face in the convent was met with approval by all, except Mother Superior. He was a little too approachable to her liking. But Clara had little choice but to accept the replacement that was sent by higher authorities.

Samuel was a big man with huge hands; he stood well over six feet tall. If it was not for his priestly attire, he would have been confused with the American actor Morgan Freeman. But what stood out starkly among his handsome features were his large black irises. They had no lustre. He had lifeless eyes. It looked as though the mirror to this priest's soul was missing. Bertha didn't give that peculiarity a second thought. But she did dwell on the fact that he offered to fly her, as her pilot, to Tswanas Kraal, even though the plan was thwarted by Mother Superior. The fuel cost for the thousand-odd-mile trip was way beyond the convent's funds. Less expensive travelling plans had to be arranged, Clara had said.

To Bertha's dismay, her mode of transport turned out to be a rickety, old van that was painted in gaudy colors designed to hide the vehicle's rust. That wasn't the worst of it, though, because halfway across the Little Karoo Desert, the brakes failed and the engine blew a gasket. The driver, who had promised Mother Superior to get Bertha safely to Tswanas, bargained with a passing nomad—an old man with an old camel. To say the least, Bertha's transport was nerve-racking and very uncomfortable. The journey to the barely accessible village—there was hardly a passable road leading down the mountain—left her body battered and bruised. But Bertha's aches and pains were soon overridden by the welcoming hospitality of the Tswanas villagers. They welcomed her royally with waves, smiles, and lots of hugs.

Bertha was escorted by a group of talkative children to a hut behind the schoolhouse that was built especially for her. Bertha wasn't surprised at the many Down syndrome children in the midst of the thronging youth. Interbreeding was not something new in these parts. But she knew she would treat all twenty of her assigned schoolchildren equally—and without interference from modern technology. Mobile phones and electricity-generating devices were not used here. It was as if Bertha had stepped back into primitive bygone days. And she liked it that way.

After washing up and making a quick change, Bertha joined the villagers for supper. She was the first to be dished goat stew that had been prepared from a poor creature slaughtered just before her arrival.

As time marched on, Bertha could not have been more content with life in the kraal. However, there were times, late at night, when she found herself overcome by desolate feelings of incompleteness … emptiness … a loneliness that she couldn't easily explain away. On these sleepless occasions, her thoughts focused on the young couples in the kraal—their loving, touchy gestures and their sexual togetherness, both of which provoked in her the image of Father Samuel. She imagined his handsome face. She envisioned his sonorous voice, an alluringly seductive voice that she had heard many times during services. She had no idea where these feelings were leading.

Then late one night, when the heavens had lost a grip on the day's scorching heat, Bertha sat on the ground outside her hut and pictured his strong male arms hugging her close. She felt his hot breath and was intoxicated by the power of his aftershave. But there was something missing from this picture. Sister Bertha knew nothing about sexual arousal; all she knew were the butterfly feelings in her gut that suggested an unfamiliar world.

Bertha was totally naive. She had not read lurid novels or watched explicit movies. She had no inkling of the ineffable communication between two bodies in love. She had never experienced the tender fondling of breasts or the gentle attentions of a lover who arouses an overpowering desire for entry into her body. This warm-blooded woman did not know that genital mutilation would never permit her to experience sexual gratification. Tragically, she would find this out the hard way. Something was going to go awry.

During other restless nights like this, Bertha jumped out of bed, angry at herself for allowing these sinful thoughts to divert her from her vow to be married only to Christ. Envisioning the wrath of Christ, she would reach for a rope-whip and flog herself in penance. This devout woman had lost track of the number of times she had flogged herself.

Soon it was time for Bertha's first Christmas breakaway from the kraal.

She arrived by bus two days before Christmas Eve, 1997. In a way, she was pleased to be back in her old stomping grounds in Nairobi, but somehow she had forgotten the drill. She was not thrilled with the constant written and, sometimes, verbal orders: "Go here ... Go there ... Pick up this ... Pick up that ... Fetch so and so."

Despite the constant orders, Sister Bertha's chore-filled, silent-filled days passed quickly, and soon the time approached for her to return to Tswanas to reopen the school. The day before her departure, January 6, 1998, Bertha was assigned her last errand. Sister Anne, the convent's main cook, asked Bertha to go out and buy onions and lentils for the evening meal's soup.

There, at the crowded marketplace, when she was not looking where she was going, Bertha literally bumped into someone she had not planned on seeing or speaking to. The vows of silence taken by the residents of the Nairobi convent prohibited conversation with *anyone* outside of its walls, but words spilled out of Bertha anyway. "Oh, I'm sorry, Father," she flustered. "I should have been minding my feet. What are you doing here? I was informed you were sent away to further your theological studies."

Samuel bent his head and scanned her face. "Ah, it's you, Sister Bertha," he said smiling broadly. "I didn't recognize you at first. You are looking well ..." He sighed. "You have no idea how much you've been missed."

Bertha stopped a frown from forming. Yes, it was a strange comment. Was he referring to her fellow nuns or to himself? She didn't dwell on it. Nor did she question the unethical familiarity of the holy man, whose hand now latched firmly onto hers. The electrifying shock of their touching hands was euphoric. Bertha's heart was beating fast as she drank in the seductive voice of her daydreams. "How are things going, Sister?" Samuel asked. "Have you perfected the Zulu language? What's Tswanas Kraal like? Is it still as primitive as I've been told? How's the teaching coming along? If you don't mind me saying so, you have a glow about you. Living in Zululand must agree with you. Have we more good souls for God? How long are you staying with us?"

Samuel's nonstop questioning brought a warm smile to Sister's Bertha's full mouth. But glares from passersby brought her back to Earth, and she quickly wiped it off. She hurriedly withdrew her hand from his and hoped that her capillary-flushed cheeks weren't going to shame her—or that God wasn't going to strike her down dead for being happy to be so close to a man.

"Let me buy you a glass of lemonade, Sister." Samuel turned slightly and gestured to a market stall with a grass roof that provided shade. "Over there. They make the finest lemonade ever."

Sister Bertha's brain numbed momentarily; then a guarded, proper reply escaped, "Thank you, Father, for the offer, but I really must get back. Sister Anne sent me to buy lentils. I'm already running late."

With an impish grin, Samuel replied, "Another time, then. I will hold you to it."

Bertha, in a daze, spun around and hurriedly left the marketplace (without the lentils) as if her life depended on it. She imagined his eyes following her for what seemed an eternity. Oh, how she would have loved to sip lemonade ever so slowly and embrace every moment spent with him. But the charismatic, mild-mannered priest was not all he seemed to be.

As Bertha neared the convent, the heavens opened up and let loose a loud roar of thunder. The "crash" was quickly followed by buckets of rain streaming down the road like a swollen river. As the rain poured, Bertha's thoughts cascaded into self-accusation: "You see? God the Father is angry with you. The rains aren't due for another month." Her self-chastising voice continued relentlessly: "How could you have been so brazen? Shame on you! Have you forgotten that you are a bride of Christ?"

Bertha was reciting Hail Mary for the umpteenth time when she entered the convent through a side door. Standing near the large cooking range was Sister Anne. "Have you brought my lentils ...?" She paused to look at Bertha, who abruptly clamped her mouth shut. "Is something the matter, Sister Bertha? You look flustered. Did the heat get to you? Come sit down. I'll pour you a glass of the tasty lemonade I've just made."

That did it. Bertha fled the kitchen.

In her nine-by-nine-foot cell, she flung herself onto her hard cot, buried her face into a pillow, and retreated deep inside herself. It was the first time since entering these convent walls that she asked herself why, "Why have I chosen the path of celibacy?"

The turmoil in her mind, brought on by the feelings aroused in her by Samuel's attention, led her to an understanding that she was an attractive woman with strong feelings for the opposite sex. Had she the *right* to feel this way? Had she the *right* to fall in love? After all, she was a warm-hearted woman, not a cold statue! Or was she just plain wicked in God's eyes?

The next morning, January 7, with her undergarments sticking to her whipped flesh, Bertha entered the private chapel. The cat-o'-nine-tails had left deep welts, but those were the least of her discomforts. She tried hard not to look at Samuel as he recited Mass for a fellow nun who had passed away in the night. To Bertha's horror, his hand stroked her cheek a little longer than expected as he administered the wafer. "The Body of Christ ..." Her thunderous heartbeat drowned out the prayer. She clung to her rosary beads as if her life depended on it.

After Mass, at the breakfast table, Bertha hardly ate a morsel. Her appetite was further curtailed when Mother Superior rose from her chair and broke the code of breakfast silence announcing, "You all know that Sister Bertha is leaving us tomorrow and returning to Tswanas. Let us pray for her safe journey."

After the inaudible mumblings of individual prayers, Clara turned to Bertha and said, "Oh, by the way, you won't have to endure such arduous travel as before. Bless him. Father Samuel has kindly offered to fly you back after ..."

The clatter of metal hitting the stone floor punctuated Clara's sentence.

Bertha quickly bent down and scooped up the half-eaten, lumpy porridge. With the bowl and contents at the ready, she straightened. Placing the dish on the table as if nothing had happened, she unthinkingly blurted, "Oh, how clumsy of me,

Sisters and Mother Superior. It won't happen again."

Their astonished looks impelled Bertha to place a hand over her mouth. She had *spoken*. This was *forbidden* at mealtimes. Only Mother Superior had that privilege.

Bertha bowed her head, acknowledging her mistake.

Clara and the other nuns bobbed their heads in acceptance.

It was past midnight when Sister Bertha finally retired to her bed. She had spent hours prostrate on the cold floor of the chapel praying for a miracle, waiting for a sign, until exhaustion had overcome her.

She awoke at her usual time of four o'clock. She washed herself with cold water, dressed in a freshly laundered habit, and headed to the chapel for morning prayers. In the quiet of this holy room, Bertha again asked for a miracle: "Please, Christ, change these plans. The Devil is trying to snatch my good soul—tempting me with the flesh of a man."

Shortly thereafter, Father Samuel awaited her arrival in a pickup truck. His face was scrubbed clean. His hair shone with whatever he had used to smooth down stray hairs, and his excessive use of cheap aftershave pervaded the interior of the vehicle.

After her goodbyes on a sunny start to the New Year, a nervous Bertha got into the truck. Was the feeling of foreboding in the pit of her stomach trying to tell her something? Did the brakes work in this old jalopy? Would her beating heart betray her? Looking straight ahead, she said in her best voice, "Good morning, Father Samuel. It is kind of you to fly me to Zululand."

"No problem, Sister. It's a pleasure."

Bertha sat as upright and stiff as a cardboard box. She hardly said a word, except in response: "Yes, it is a fine day for flying, Father ... No, I've never flown before ... Yes, I'm nervous ... But I'm in good hands, thank you."

Samuel laughed. "Don't be nervous. I'm the best bush pilot out here. But before we get to the airstrip, I have to make a stop at my apartment to collect an overnight bag. Come up, if you like, and give me your honest opinion." He cleared his throat. "Maybe you could suggest what color paint I should use on my walls."

Instantly, Bertha's gut instinct screamed: "No, no, no." But her love-struck heart overruled logic, and out rushed her impulsive response, "I can do that for you, Father. I do have a keen eye for color."

Inside Samuel's modest home, Bertha felt an uneasy feeling grip her stomach. She had never been in a man's apartment before, and she knew in her heart it wasn't right. Then suddenly, a cold chill ran down her spine. She started to leave … make an excuse … return to the truck …

Samuel's asphyxiating chokehold left Bertha fighting for air in voiceless helplessness. In survival mode, her hands fought to loosen the fierce grip on her neck. Even with a good dose of adrenaline kicking in, she was no match for Samuel's muscular strength. As she was pushed to the floor, Bertha, her head spinning, felt her life slipping away. She wanted to scream, but the words on the tip of her tongue hung silently: "This is wrong, Father. Please stop. In God's name, please stop."

In the darkest zone of mankind, Bertha blacked out. Mercifully, her unconsciousness took the assaulted nun to another place and time.

After what seemed an eternity, Bertha's pain-gummed eyes opened. Disorientated, she tried to take in the unfamiliar surroundings. Where was she? Why was she in a strange room? Why did she feel like she had been run over by a train? She heard what sounded like faraway voices, but one was raised and very agitated. "You raped a *nun!*" the man said in outraged disbelief as he gestured at the crumpled habit on the bedroom floor. This sickening discovery left the enraged man momentarily numb. Then he turned to the perpetrator for answers. "Prostitutes are one thing—but a nun! Are you out of your mind?"

Samuel twitched, looked down, and muttered, "Oh, no! I can't believe I did that."

Doctor William Ungobo, age fifty-two, shook his head. What had brought this man of God down a slippery slope to the point of no return? Could demonic possession be the cause? The man of science wasn't convinced. William—a comforting, grandfatherly figure with warm hazel eyes—was determined to get to the truth this time. Yes, there had been a pattern of attacks on women, and the person responsible for this latest horrendous crime was his *own* son. Sick to his stomach, William vented, "I'm a physician, not a psychiatrist! I can't heal your twisted, psychotic brain. If I wasn't your father, I would call the police and have your sorry ass thrown in jail! This is the last time, Samuel. Do I make myself clear?"

Samuel's reply was inaudible.

Just as well. He would have lied anyway, smiling while doing so. And there was nothing his father could do or say. The beatings Samuel had received as a rebellious child by his disciplinary father were long done.

In the hair-trigger atmosphere of the room, the tension could have been cut with a knife.

William, his medical bag clutched in one hand, walked over to Bertha, who was lying on the single bed. The doctor had instructed Samuel to pick her up from the floor and lay her there. On visual examination William noted the contusions to the nun's face, eyes, and mouth; strangulation marks on her neck; and defensive bruises on her hands. But Bertha's medical caregiver was not prepared for her worst injury.

The board-certified gynecologist and obstetrician lifted Bertha's limp hand. Avoiding her intense gaze, William addressed his patient. "I know it is little consolation for what you have been through, but I'm very sorry this has happened to you." He placed his free hand to his heart. "I'm a doctor, and I need to examine you." From behind them, Samuel was muttering, "A demon possesses me. Exorcism … expulsion … whatever it takes. I have to be healed."

Although excruciating pain was burning through her body like hot, flowing lava, Bertha, her nakedness a humiliation in the presence of two men, drew her knees up in a fetal position, closed her eyes, and silently prayed. She did not utter a sound or move a muscle while the physician's cold hands parted her rigid legs. The steady flow of blood was worrisome to the doctor. On closer examination, he noted the cause. He stepped away from his patient and grabbed Samuel roughly by the shoulder. In a low but angry voice, William delivered this chilling statement, "She is tribally circumcised, you idiot! She's lost a lot of blood and needs hospital treatment."

"She *can't* go to the hospital," Samuel protested. "They will call the police."

William paid no heed to Samuel's retort and concentrated on Bertha's condition. It wouldn't be the first time that he had examined a circumcised woman whose labia minora had been sealed with crude stitching. In those patients, normal intercourse caused penetration bleeding, but not extensively. In Bertha's case, she had been forcefully *raped*. Without a doubt, the nature of her vaginal tearing and facial bruising would result in the ER doctor calling the police.

The doctor was torn.

As he covered Bertha's naked body with a bedspread, his

thoughts overpowered him. He couldn't take her to his own private clinic, either. It was his professional duty to report a rape, and the nun's presence would not escape the keen eye of his nurse, a former nun herself, who lived in the apartment above the clinic. Indecision ripped into the doctor's moral compass. He wanted to strangle this son he had so lovingly nurtured after the death of his wife. Instead, the father in him cautioned his son aloud. "If you don't put an end to your despicable behavior, you are going to wind up in a six-by-six prison cell. And I'm not going to cover your ass like I've done with the prostitutes you have raped and beaten in the past. Do you understand?"

Samuel covered his face with his hands and repeatedly mumbled under his breath: "I'm an animal. I'm an animal. No, I'm worse than an animal."

William's eyes blazed with disgust. "You are the lowest form of *human* life. Oh, I'm so glad that your mother isn't here to see how her only son turned out—a devil in sheep's clothing. May her good soul rest in peace, and with God's help may the soul of this holy woman be healed." He gulped hard. "And you had better start praying that *she* doesn't report you."

"She won't," was Samuel's icy response. He blew a guttural raspberry.

William didn't know how to react to that statement or Samuel's childlike behavior. But in this case the moral overtone was this: *The bad guy did wear black.* There was no doubt in the doctor's mind that his son was sick in the head—living in a world without truth or consequence. Surely, though, he was not a murderer.

The medical caregiver returned to Bertha, who had her hands up over her head. Without a word, he opened his black bag and removed a sterile suture needle, catgut, and antiseptic rubbing alcohol. Her pain-filled cries stuck to the ceiling like a fresh coat of plaster as the cold, sharp stitching needle stabbed her flesh. She felt as if she was being victimized all over again.

William's heart was near breaking. He was in torment. He didn't want to abandon the nun like he had previously done with the street workers. But were they any different than the Sister? No, they were all victims. Against William's better judgment, Samuel's latest target would have to ride out this storm by herself. His hopes for her full recovery were made in a silent prayer: "Dear God, watch over your servant. Heal her wounds. Heal her heart and fill it with forgiveness."

Samuel left Bertha with an internal wound that would never heal. Would she ever be able to trust a male again? Would her external and internal wounds heal? Only time had the answer to those questions.

William removed a syringe and a small glass vial from his bag. He ripped the protective covering off of the syringe, filled it, and injected Bertha in her right buttock. She grabbed his hand and tearfully pleaded, "Please, don't leave me here. Take me with you. I know he is your son. I won't tell anyone. Honest to God, I promise."

Fighting back his own tears, William replied, "Forgive me, Sister. I can't do that." He turned his back and pulled Samuel aside. In a whisper he said, "I've given her a good dose of antibiotics, just in case you have transmitted the bacterial vaginosis you got from the last prostitute. Make sure she takes the rest of the pills I've left on the bedside table."

The broken-hearted doctor turned on his heels, slammed the door shut, and stormed down the stairway toward the fresh air. In his heart of hearts, William hoped never to see his son again, but something told him that wasn't going to happen. If it were not for the fear of losing his good name, his small medical practice, and the income which was barely enough to sustain his new wife and baby daughter, he would have gladly reported Samuel to the police. William knew the time would come sooner than later for him to repair the cracks in his own moral compass. He must end this unnatural alliance with his son, because although the doctor didn't want to admit it, Samuel was a serial rapist, and William wanted nothing more to do with him.

But the past has a way of clawing its way back. The lives of William, Bertha, and Samuel would cross again.

Bertha groaned in pain on Samuel's bed. Her private parts felt like they had been broiled. Her hand touched the catgut, and she began to weep loudly. Samuel rushed to her side. Bertha was not expecting contriteness. "Please forgive me, Bertha. I don't know what came over me. All I can say is that it was the Devil's doing. I will go to confession and beg God's forgiveness."

Bertha chose not to respond. As a woman, not the nun, she could choose the dark path of wrath or the path of forgiveness. Naturally, she blamed herself for what happened. She considered the consequences if she chose to report her rapist. She would have to endure a hospital examination, police questioning, and even possible media scrutiny. Worst would be the grilling she would receive from the church's legal authorities and the unpleasant dispositions by both the prosecutor and defense lawyer. If the court failed her and did not convict Samuel and send him to jail, then she would be confined to the convent walls for the rest of her natural life, never able to see the outside world again. These thoughts filled her with dread, pain, and shame.

Suddenly, Bertha had an emotional breakthrough. A picture in her mind of the Tswanas children eagerly awaiting her return after the Christmas break decided the matter for her. No, she couldn't let this horrible event interfere with her future. No, she would not remain sitting in a corner crying. She was not a victim. She was a survivor. And no, this life-shattering experience was not going to psychologically claim what was left of her life.

In the end, perpetually optimistic Bertha chose to believe that good would triumph over evil. Yes, she knew what had happened to her was not *love*. And although she felt betrayed by her Maker, she blamed herself. But just as she had done as a child, after she had survived horrifying violence in her village, she resolved that this latest brutality would not end the teaching life she loved. She could not let the rape defeat her. She refused to hate. If she wanted to move on, she would have to forgive. That would be a tall order. So the only way to be at peace was to pretend the rape never happened. Everybody has something to hide and the courageous Bertha would hide hers well.

"If the blow doesn't kill you, it will strengthen you," Bertha uttered with conviction.

It was a definitive moment in Bertha's life.

Her mother, Nthara, must have been smiling from Heaven because her "special" daughter, Farida, was, indeed, being reborn.

CHAPTER SIX

Tswanas Kraal, mid-February 1998

IT WAS A MUGGY AFTERNOON, and a distinctive earthy smell clung to the air following the brief thunderstorm. In summer, with hot days and warm balmy nights, it wasn't unusual for such a thunderstorm to let loose and then quickly clear.

At the riverbank, Sister Bertha was laundering her smalls. When she heard an unfamiliar rumbling, she looked heavenward. Seeing nothing, she gave no further thought to the sound and returned to the chore at hand. Bertha had no clue that a helicopter was bringing a stranger to these parts. Tswanas seldom had visitors, and certainly not by this method of modern transport. Unknown to Bertha this particular visitor would forever be part of her natural life.

A safe distance from the helicopter rotor blades, Lynette Martinez, age fifty-three—also known by her African name, Shiya—bent down and, with the flat of her hand, brushed off a layer of whipped-up dirt that had settled on the legs of her white Levi jeans. Her elderly escort, Kelingo, smiled while thinking, "Why on Earth did she choose to wear white clothing in the African bush? It's beyond reason." But then, in his estimation, white people were strange, period.

Kelingo sidled up to the woman and said, "I'm sorry for the way that awful man treated you. I hope you understand that it's not my place to get involved in arguments between white folk."

Shiya draped an arm around her escort's shoulders and responded, "Good Lord, there's no need for *you* to apologize, old chap." She awaited a response. None came. But she could see by his long face that her apology was not enough. It was obvious that he wanted to get something more off his chest. Shiya patted his shoulder. "Do you want to tell me about it, Kelingo?"

Without a second thought Kelingo opened up: "I was a very, very happy man when Nelson Mandela was freed and appointed to be our president. After the abolishment of apartheid, I had hoped that things would improve between our races. Sadly, that's not the case. I have witnessed firsthand how racial hatred continues to stick to the hearts of both black and white folk—more now than ever."

Shiya wanted to agree with him, to open her heart to the suffering of others, but she had been gone a long while. She knew from childhood experiences that racial hatred could only be dissolved if the person who hated had moral conviction. But now was not the time to continue the conversation. She sighed. "I would love to carry on this conversation further, Kelingo, but it will have to wait because I'm eager to see Anele." At that moment she felt like pinching herself. She could not believe she was actually stepping back in time to the place where she had spent the first years of her life. Unable to contain her emotions, Shiya ran forward hollering, "Whoopee! I'm home at last!"

Kelingo's old eyes smiled warmly. He too was happy to be in his homeland.

While moving ahead of Kelingo, eager to reach their destination, Shiya turned and asked, "How much farther is it?"

"Not that far now."

"Great. But these darn shoes are killing me." Shiya bent down and removed her sandals. She flung them to the side of the dirt pathway. "Whoever finds them is welcome to them," she mumbled.

Kelingo, with the skin of his forehead stretched high, stared after the discarded footwear. He shook his head and said, "It's not wise to go barefoot here, unless you have leathery old feet like mine that nothing can penetrate. There are lots of poisonous thorns, centipedes, and fire ants that would be happy to bite into your soft feet."

With an impish grin, Shiya countered, "The buggers won't like the taste of my blood. My feet will just have to get leathery like yours."

The excited woman skipped along the pathway like a sprightly teenager until a stabbing pain halted her in her tracks. "Ouch! What the ..." The expletive was inaudible, but not her voiced pain: "Ow," she groaned. She lifted her leg to inspect her foot. And there they were—a bunch of thorn barbs embedded into her heel and arch, and they were protruding like shards of fine glass.

Kelingo wanted to say, "I told you so," but he thought better of it. His experienced fingers plucked out the thorny attackers. Shiya never uttered a sound. Kelingo, trying to keep a straight face, handed Shiya her footwear. She gave him a sheepish "thank you."

Shiya, her feet now shielded from the nasties of the African bush, sprinted down a well-trodden pathway. Her green eyes were dancing with joy when, at last, she spotted thatched roofs.

A childhood memory flashed: the spanking Anele had given her for climbing over the kraal gate when she was about four years old. Anele had warned, "Shiya! You won't be able to sit down for a week if you do that again. There are dangers out there that a child knows nothing about!"

The reflection faded and, with newfound happiness, Shiya marvelled at her surroundings. "Yes, this is where I left my heart."

Shiya's presence at the gate sent the village dogs into a barking frenzy. With teeth bared and saliva drooling, they rushed toward the fence. Shiya shooed them off and fumbled with the rope hitch. When no one from the inside came to her aid, she looked back for Kelingo, who was nowhere in sight. "Has he stopped to relieve himself?"

With impatience overriding logic, and with the most unladylike movements, Shiya clambered to the top of the wooden-slatted fence, lost her balance, and landed flat on her backside into a fresh cowpat. Spattered with manure, she was at first mortified, and then began to laugh to the point of tears.

Kelingo suddenly appeared. He had no problem undoing the latch. He clapped a hand over his mouth to muffle his giggles. Shiya scowled playfully and then said, "Please feel free to laugh your head off, Kelingo. I should have waited for you."

Kelingo offered Shiya his hand. "Here, let me help you up." After he pulled her to her feet, Shiya wiped her dirty hands on the sides of her white jeans and muttered, "Oh, this is a fine way to meet my family."

By now many of the villagers, mostly women, had surrounded the visitors. Some of the adults had curious frowns on their faces, while the kids snickered and pointed their fingers. A stocky, elderly woman pushed her way through the crowd. A broad smile creased her chapped lips as she greeted her sibling. "Brother Kelingo, my heart sings with joy at your unexpected presence!"

Shiya couldn't stand the suspense a moment longer. "Kelingo, my Zulu is rusty. I haven't a clue what she's saying. But please tell your people why I'm here, and take me to Anele."

To the gawking crowd of about twenty, Kelingo announced, "This is Mrs. Lynette Martinez. She has come all the way from North America to see her mother, Anele."

Expressions of disbelief appeared—mostly on the elderly.

Kelingo continued. "Some of you older folk may remember the white child who lived here for five years ..." He inhaled sharply before hitting the tribe with the revelation, "... before she and Anele were kidnapped by the white man."

A large-breasted woman elbowed her way to the front line and, with remarkable strength, nearly sucked the life out of Shiya with a fierce hug. "I didn't recognize you," the woman murmured against Shiya's cheek. "We have both grown old."

Shiya stared into the cobalt irises that were bright with emotion. Then it dawned on her, "Oh, my God! Is it really you, Maekela?"

"Yes, dear friend."

"Is Isona here, too?"

"No. Sadly, she is with our loved ones in the Invisible Kingdom. She died in childbirth many years back. But she's doing a good job in our heaven. She's caring for the many village children we have lost to disease. She is also caring for my son, who was killed a couple of years back in a diamond mine explosion. His body was never recovered, but his spirit, with Isona's help, lives through me. I feel him close each day."

"Oh, I'm so sorry to hear of your loss. But darling Maekela, please take me to my mother," pleaded a tearful Shiya. "I can't wait another moment."

Before Maekela could comply, a tall woman stepped between

them, blue eyes twinkling in the sunlight. "I've heard so much about the white baby my mother rescued. I'm thrilled to know you, my younger sister."

Shiya wore a puzzled frown. "I'm sorry," she said. "Should I know you? I don't remember Anele having another child when I was here in the kraal."

"No, you couldn't know this. You see, I was born before you were found in the corn pit in the Valley of a Thousand Hills. I was raised in Kenya by Father Batuzi and his wife, Nyasha. My name is Insikazi, which means 'fawn' in English."

It took a moment for the revelation to sink in. "Oh, my goodness. I can't believe it!" Shiya gasped. "Maekela told me that a child had been taken from Anele when she was a teenager!" Shiya's thoughts began to race. "You've got to tell me. How did *you* find Anele?"

Insikazi shook her head. "I'd love to share my story with you later, but first, I'm sorry to say that you arrived on the day that *Umama* visits the grave of her father, my grandfather, who once was chieftain of this village."

Shiya's impatience got the better of her. "Show me the way to the burial place," she urged. "I must see her. I can't wait any longer." Suddenly she remembered her appearance and laughed. "But I can't let my mother see me like this! Is there somewhere I can wash and change? I don't want Anele to think a cow with diarrhea has come to visit her!"

Insikazi laughed heartily and translated for the gawking crowd, whose laughter filled the hot air with a good dose of mirth. Then the tribe dispersed as if it were an everyday occurrence to have an *umlungu* visitor among them. Insikazi turned to Shiya and said, "By the time I get water fetched from the river for you to wash, *our mother* ..." she hesitated, smiling at the shared words, "... will probably be on her way back. Vimbela always brings her back before the sun sets. That will give you plenty of time to prepare."

Shiya scratched her chin. "Hey, that name rings a bell."

"It should because Vimbela was your wet nurse, Shiya."

Shiya's smile stretched ear to ear. She was deep in reflection when Kelingo interrupted her euphoric thoughts: "Mrs. Martinez, do you need me for anything?"

"No, Kelingo. I'll be just fine."

"Okay. Then before some animal gets to the food boxes, I'm going with some helpers to collect them."

"Kelingo, how many times do I have to remind you? For Pete's sake, no more 'Mrs. Martinez.' Out here my name is Shiya, my true name, and from now on the awful English name given to me by my stepmother is no more—not while I live here in Tswanas. I want you to call me Shiya. Okay?"

Kelingo looked at his feet. His voice was low. "I'm sorry, but I'm not accustomed to calling white people by their first names, but if you insist, Shiya is a good African name."

Shiya's heart flooded with appreciation and love for this old man who had so willingly assisted her. And she found it delightful the way he pronounced her name: *Shee-I-ya*. This new thought enhanced the warmth of her given name.

"Kelingo, when you bring back the boxes, you'll find one marked with a large 'C.' Open it first and hand out the treats for the children. I don't suppose these poor kids have ever seen candy."

His brows rose to his hairline. "*All* of the treats?"

Warm laughter rippled from Shiya's throat. "No silly! Just give each of them a lollipop for now."

"A pleasure," Kelingo responded. "I can't thank you enough for your tender heart toward our people, especially the children."

Shiya placed her hand on Kelingo's and said, "You don't need to thank me. It is you whom I should be thanking."

The old man bowed. "It has been an honor ..." he exhaled noisily.

"Spit it out, Kelingo. What is it you wish to add?"

The old man wrung his hands. "In the white man's world, I was half a man, but here in the bush, I am a whole man. I don't want to return to the law firm, but it doesn't look like Mr. Durval will let me out of my work contract even though there's less than a year of my employment remaining."

"Maybe I'll be able to work something out with Bryan to get you out of the contract."

Kelingo nodded. "I better go now."

Shiya watched Kelingo head for the gate with a bevy of boys close behind him, and then, at the same gate, she saw Anele's natural daughter hand a pail to a robust girl. Insikazi's instructions were loud and clear. "Go quickly to the river," she ordered. "Fill this to the top and bring it to my hut. Go fast, Leticia." Then Insikazi called out to Shiya, "Come. I'll take you to my home. You can undress there. When Leticia gets back, you can wash."

The two women strolled leisurely toward the cluster of a dozen or more huts at the far end of the compound. Shiya's cheeks now displayed a healthy glow underneath the dung spatter.

Her brain tumor was the furthest thing from her mind. All she needed to complete her mounting happiness was to see and hug her beloved Anele.

As they neared the huts, Insikazi pointed to two houses at the end of the mud-walled assemblage. "That one is mine, and the big one to the right is Anele's home. Do you remember it?"

"Not really," Shiya answered truthfully. The huts all looked the same to her.

As a visitor to Tswanas, Shiya was pleasantly surprised when she stepped into Insikazi's hut. Although the woman's living quarters were windowless and no bigger that an average clothes closet, the well-pounded soil was shiny and immaculate. In the center of the hut was a raised cot bed covered by a colorful, hand-stitched, patchwork quilt. Oval clay oil lamps sat on tree stumps that served as nightstands. Shiya was surprised at how neat and tidy Insikazi's hut was and was intoxicated by the smell wafting up to her nostrils. She had never smelled anything like it before. It prompted the question. "What *is* that glorious smell?"

"Oh, do you like it? It is the oil from the black ironwood trees. I sprinkle it on the floor to stop the pests—spiders, ants, dog fleas—from getting to my bed and eating me alive!"

Shiya giggled like a little girl. That would be one perfume that she would not dab behind her ears.

While awaiting the washing water, Insikazi made a pot of tea from crushed red leaves. The two women found plenty to say about trivial matters while they sipped herbal tea. But these were not the things Shiya wanted to discuss. Finally, Insikazi spoke of Anele: "Our mother is frail in body due to being so long in jail, and her eyesight is poor. But believe me, Anele's mind is sharper than the claw of an eagle. This you will find out ..."

They were interrupted by the entrance of a stooped visitor who sidled up to Shiya and introduced herself: "My name is Sister Bertha, and I'm the schoolteacher. Word reached me of your arrival while I was bathing in the river. Little Leticia can't be far behind me."

"Nice to make your acquaintance," Shiya greeted. Her eyes took in the nun's Cleopatra looks: purple-black smooth skin and twinkling onyx eyes. Shiya noticed that Sister Bertha did not have typical Zulu features: a rounded face; a broad, flattened nose; a long neck; and a high forehead.

Shiya's eagerness to know more about this interesting woman dominated the chitchat.

"You're not from these parts, are you, Sister Bertha?"

"No, I'm not. I was born in a village very similar to this one, but on the east coast of Africa."

"How did you end up here?"

"Ah, it is a long story," Bertha replied in a teasing tone. "But I can tell you that I'm happy to be here. Can I ask you how long you intend to stay here in Tswanas?"

"For the rest of what remains of my life."

Sister Bertha eyes narrowed. She waited for Shiya to explain, and when she didn't, the nun decided it would be too impolite to question the visitor further. So Bertha began to speak of the progress her students were making.

Shiya found herself warming to the dedicated nun and hoped for a sincere friendship to develop. But was this religious woman open-minded enough to be trusted? Not being worldly, could she ever understand the depth of Shiya's brutal past? Little did she know that Bertha was indeed a kindred spirit when it came to painful past secrets. Two years ago she had been defiled by the Devil himself!

Shiya gently took hold of the nun's hand and led her outside.

"Sister, I'll let you into one little secret that I hope you will keep for now. The reason I'm here is that I have a tumor growing on my brain that will shorten my life. So you see, I've come home to reclaim my foster mother and my lost childhood before I can no longer remember."

Bertha's dark eyes moistened as she responded to Shiya's revelation, "Oh, I'm so sorry. I will pray for you. If there is anything I can do to help you, please don't hesitate to ask. I hope we can become close friends. I'd like to make your stay here a happy one.

Let me assure you, your secret is safe with me."

"Thanks, Sister. I'm looking forward to having some wonderful chats with you over a cup of tea."

Shiya happened to glance down at Bertha's feet. Her patched black shoes had trod more miles than could be expected of them. The observation triggered Shiya into action. "Before you go, Sister, I've got something for you. Wait here a moment." Shiya dashed inside and retrieved her sandals. "Your feet look about the same size as mine, so I'd like you to have these."

"Oh ... mmm ... th-ank you," the nun stammered, clutching the footwear to her chest. Bertha's expression shone with gratitude. She dug deep into her tunic pocket, removed a small silver crucifix, and handed it to Shiya. "And I'd like you to have this. He will protect you."

Shiya stared at the gift, and then, out of character, got prickly. "No bloody thanks. I don't bloody want it. I've had more than my fill of Catholicism without being reminded of it."

Shiya's insensitivity distressed Bertha. Her eyes filled with tears.

"I didn't mean ..." Shiya felt horrible. She could have kicked herself for not biting her tongue. She tried to undo the damage by saying, "Oh, I'm sorry, Sister. I didn't mean to be rude or ungrateful. Find someone who truly deserves your religious gesture." Once more, Shiya didn't weigh her words. "You see, Bertha, I don't bloody believe in God."

Bertha smiled in a way that told Shiya this holy woman would not give up trying to convert her. She obviously had high expectations. But like the Jehovah's Witnesses who continually turned up on Shiya's doorstep in Canada—to a closed door, that is—Bertha would receive the same treatment if she was persistent.

Waving goodbye, Bertha headed to the schoolhouse, and Shiya

went back indoors. Sitting cross-legged on the floor in Insikazi's hut, Shiya dismissed her rude behavior and felt perfectly at home. It felt as though she'd never left this village of her childhood and had never lived in relative luxury. All thoughts of her post-village life—creature comforts, her brain condition, and the loved ones she'd left behind—vanished from her mind as if waved away by a sorcerer's wand. Her return to the village was so important to her, second only to the birth of her daughter, Brianna—because soon she would be seeing the woman who had saved her from an awful death and had become the only mother she had ever known.

CHAPTER SEVEN

Holy Cross School, Soweto Township, December 2009

SISTER BERTHA SAT AT HER DESK on this Tuesday school morning, and without reason, she found herself overpowered by a blitz of horrible reflections that dragged her back to her childhood and to other dark days in her former life. Even after so many years the emotional pain, the sting of her haunting past endured. Today, she felt like she was falling into a well of murky waters. As far as Bertha knew, she was her immediate family's only survivor, and she took full credit for her life and healing. But ever since the massacre of her tribespeople, not a day had gone by without her questioning why. Bertha dropped to her knees, clasped her hands in prayer, and turned her tear-filled eyes heavenward. She begged her Maker to relieve her of the ghastly memories.

The nun's prayer went unanswered. Horrific pictures, sounds, and smells bombarded her consciousness. Bertha fought the tears, but the awful recollections were too much for her. It was mental torture at its cruellest. Bertha sobbed into her hands. Fortunately, her assistant was nowhere in sight. Claudia was washing up the breakfast dishes.

After Bertha's spirit felt thoroughly drowned, she stood up, wiped her face with the hem of her tunic, and as if nothing had caused her to fall to her knees, headed to the kitchenette at the rear of the schoolhouse. There she addressed her assistant in a composed, professional voice: "It's nearly nine o'clock, Sister Claudia. Ring the school bell, please, and let the little angels enter."

Sister Bertha collected enough strength to smile warmly, even though the clanging of the schoolteacher's brass bell did nothing to relieve her pounding headache. In a way, though, she was thankful for the clamor because it brushed away her suffocating thoughts and instantly relieved her emotional pressure.

As her energy began to increase, Bertha did a hop and a skip to the chalkboard. She loved her job. Educating children and teaching them God's Word is what she lived for. Or so she thought. But on this very day, her unshakeable faith would be challenged. There was a psychic storm on the horizon. It would rock the core of her Christian beliefs.

Sister Bertha opened a drawer in her desk and removed a large package of different flavored lollipops. She slit the cellophane packaging with a pocketknife. The fruity fragrance wafted up to her nostrils. She was tempted to put one candy aside for herself, but instead shook her head. Her sweet tooth would have to wait. She knew these carbohydrate treats composed much of the daily sustenance of the majority of her children. She had to distribute the sweets fairly and evenly.

At that moment, Bertha made a mental note to ask once more for the additional funding needed to provide at least one hot meal a day for these children. But Bertha shrugged pessimistically. She sensed her request would be met with the same response she had received when she asked to increase the operating budget for the displaced Tswanas tribespeople. "Sister," the Father had said, "as much as I admire your compassionate heart, you know as well as I do that money does not grow on trees! You have a restricted budget because money is needed for medicine for the AIDS epidemic … blah … blah … blah."

With clenched lips, Bertha held back the desire to give him a piece of her mind: "If money grew on trees, Father, I wouldn't be standing here begging, now would I?"

Whenever Bertha had asked the church for top-up expenses, she had received the same proverbial answer: "Money doesn't grow on trees." She recalled the day the game reserve officials had presented the Tswanas tribe a forty-eight hour eviction notice and, at the same time, handed Bertha, who had been appointed to oversee the tribe's move, a paltry compensation sum. The cash barely covered the bus fare, food, and rents that had to be met when the tribespeople arrived at their new living quarters.

While the children made their way to their individual desks, Bertha's thoughts continued to travel back in time. Just three days ago, she was assisting the evicted tribespeople start new lives in Soweto after helping them—some eighty in number—onto the game reserve bus for an eight-and-a-half-hour drive to their new location. At the time Bertha had unshakeable faith that God would make this relocation painless. *He* would guide them all safely. But to her horror, two babies strapped to their mothers' backs died of heatstroke in the non-air conditioned transport, and two elderly women succumbed into unconsciousness. Toddlers clung to their mothers' knees, while older children, who were squeezed onto the hard seats next to their parents, merely accepted their uprooting as an adventure. A few of the children ran up and down the aisle of the moving bus, much to the driver's annoyance. He yelled for order, "Sit down, or I will stop the bus and make you get off."

And now, more memories flooded into her mind. In response to the driver's frustration, Bertha rose from her own hard bus seat and quickly handed out paper and crayons to the restless children, saying, "I know it's hard to sit for such a long time, but the bus driver has to get us to your new home safely, and he won't be able to concentrate if you are running up and down the aisle."

When the bus finally rolled into the township, Bertha noticed that some of the faces on her fellow passengers were blank with shock at what they saw. She could only imagine what they were thinking. Yes, back home in the kraal their living conditions were primitive, but here the smell of decomposition, as well as the sight of rundown slum shacks, litter-strewn streets, and the morose looks of the Soweto inhabitants who were staring at them brought many a fearful gasp. An elderly woman sitting on an aisle seat latched onto Bertha's arm. "What is this place? Why have you brought us to the witch doctor's underworld?"

Another woman piped up, "Take us back home! I would rather die than live here."

Bertha's heart sighed, but she could only speak of the official orders: "If I had an alternative, I never would have brought you here, but living here is not that bad. I will help all of you to adjust. I promise."

Some heads nodded complacently, some lowered in defeat, while others shook in dissatisfaction.

Sister Bertha was the first to get off the bus. As the tribespeople stepped down to follow her, the holy woman began a head count. "Maybe I'm wrong but we are one short," Bertha said to the bus driver. She re-counted, and then it hit her—"Vimbela! *Where is Vimbela?*"

Frantically, Bertha shot back onto the bus. She checked above and under every seat. It was common knowledge that when Vimbela was frightened she hid wherever she could. On many past occasions, she had to be coaxed down from a baobab tree outside the kraal.

Bertha felt as if she was sitting on a chair with one leg and was being thrown off balance. She wanted to slap herself. How could she have missed *this* woman who could hardly walk or see? And yet, Bertha recalled seeing her standing at the end of the line to get onto the bus. The last thing Bertha wanted was for this afflicted person to be left behind only to be discovered by the wild creatures that were being introduced to the new game reserve. The nun made up her mind that as soon as she settled the other tired souls, she would return to Tswanas and search for Vimbela, who had stolen the hearts of Anele, Shiya, and herself. For the time being, though, Bertha had to first deal with her obligatory commitment to settle the dislocated in Soweto.

Although the tribespeople were accustomed to poverty, the strung-together tin shacks were a shock to them. These homes were nothing like the sturdy straw and dung homes they had spent their lives in. The Tswanas tribe couldn't have known that Sister Bertha had sought out the landlord before their arrival. He had been merciless. "That's my price. Take it or leave it."

With no other choice, Sister Bertha had agreed to the exorbitant rents. "Here. Please accept this as a deposit," she said, handing the landlord an envelope containing half of the game reserve compensation cash.

Mandegizi, the machine operator who had come to excavate the Tswanas burial ground, would have had a fit if he had learned that his eldest brother, Konoye, was a rental crook. In order to own and keep these shanties, Konoye, the black sheep of the family, had been pilfering from the monthly allowance Mandegizi had been giving to their mother. Mrs. Umdaba was fully aware of her troubled son's thievery, but she chose to ignore it. After all, Konoye was her favorite child!

An hour later, God's emissary, Sister Bertha, spent what was left of the remaining daylight hours on Friday placing ten people in each of the eight rentals until better housing and more funding became available. Then she set off for the grocery store.

There, Bertha asked for credit to purchase the bulk supplies for the displaced tribespeople. Without hesitation, the Catholic storekeeper agreed and said, "Pay me when you can, Sister. If there is anything else you need, please let me know."

Not everyone in this shanty town was crook.

Bertha spent what was left of the weekend visiting each rental to make sure the tribe had settled. She then returned to the schoolhouse to prepare for her Monday morning class. The missing Vimbela was not on her list of things to do. Had Sister Bertha's hectic frame of mind so overwhelmed her that Vimbela's plight was simply forgotten? In a nearby shack, there was another woman who could never be forgotten.

As the sun set on Sunday evening, a couple of homes away from the tribe's allotted shacks, a frail woman, looking worn and old, stood in her doorway with her hand clamped over her mouth. Umia of Tswanas never thought she would reunite with her people, but there was no mistaking the traditional face markings and ear piercings she saw. These people *were* the Tswanas tribe. What were they doing here? Would any of them recognize her? Her banishment from the kraal had taken place sixty-four years ago, when she was a teenager, not long after the birth of her first child. She was sure no one would notice her now.

Umia was not the fine figure of an African maiden she had

once been. Her formerly majestic head of thick hair was dreadfully thin; her multiple ear piercings lay naked; her neck adornments were a thing of the past; and her henna-dyed tribal markings had faded long ago. But there was something Umia could not hide. Her cheeks and neck had enlarged volcanic ulcerations—the telltale signs. She was HIV positive.

Umia, with scrawny, drooping shoulders, slunk back into her shack and sat on a hard rustic chair made of twigs. Hidden away in the corner of her mind was an emotional pain like Bertha's that Umia had tried to forget. As she closed her eyes, many memories collided in her head reflecting the days when her life had been the happiest, before the day that had changed everything. Remembering Anele's angry face was more than Umia could handle. Nervous perspiration pooled on her upper lip. With her bony back pressed tight against the rear of the chair, she clasped her hands over her face.

Most human beings do not want to burden themselves with the tragedies of the past, but the memories that had shaped her unfortunate life began to involuntarily spill forth. "I remember everything … I can forget nothing," Umia murmured. If it hadn't been for the ill-fated return of Chief Naboto's daughter, Anele, in the year of 1945, she never would have ended up on this cold, dirt floor totally dependent on her young grandchild for her everyday needs.

"Why, oh why was I so stupid?" she bewailed. "Life could have been so different, if I hadn't …"

The past swallowed Umia whole. Unfortunately, in her trip down her rabbit hole, she found no magical *Alice in Wonderland* fantasy awaiting her.

The future would be unforgiving.

CHAPTER EIGHT

Tswanas Kraal, Zululand, Umia's story, 1945-2009

ON THIS LATE DECEMBER EVENING, the sun was close to setting, and the air was finally cooling. Inside her parents' hut, Vimbela's half-sister, Umia, a wholesome fourteen-year-old girl (who, unlike Vimbela, did not have Down syndrome), placed her drowsy newborn, just five hours old, in his makeshift bassinet, a reed-woven basket. Lying on his back, the baby boy slumbered. Umia yawned. She was exhausted. But the teen mother would not enjoy a well-earned nap. She had chores to catch up on before her parents returned from searching for edible tubers and mushrooms for their evening meal.

Sweeping the hut of evening creatures—spiders and other unwanted bushland pests—was a must. Making sure the oil lamps were filled before dark was another must. Ensuring that a bucket was filled with cooking water was vital, and that meant a hurried trek to the river before darkness robbed her of the pathway. Umia yawned again. She was exhausted. But a pressing need sent her outdoors.

As she squatted at the back of the hut to relieve her bladder, the hullabaloo—a storm of frenzied barking—deafened her ears. It wasn't unusual for the pack of village dogs to growl at anything that moved outside the compound. Leopards and hyenas frequently stalked the perimeters of the settlement at dusk in search of an easy meal. In the midst of the current continuous fracas, human wailing could be heard.

Umia rushed back to her hut to see her baby's arms and legs flailing. She cradled her child. "I would like to strangle the dogs," she growled. "It's okay," she soothed. "*Umama* is here."

Hours earlier, with her mother's help, the teenager had brought her first child into the world. Not unlike Nthara's birth experience delivering Bertha, it should have been the happiest moment in Umia's life, but it was not. The pleased first-time mother proudly presented her husband, Ithunzi, with the healthy full-term son she had named after him. But one moment she had a husband, and the next she was a bush-widow, of sorts.

After learning he had fathered a child two months after marriage, Ithunzi Senior, age fifteen, realized he now had to support three people. But how? The village depended on their crops for their livelihood, and it had been a bad year—months of drought had seen to that. So he had resigned himself—a man's got to do what a man's got to do—and decided that he couldn't support his family if he stayed with the tribe. His decision to leave the village and work in the gold mines was not well met. "You can't leave me," Umia had cried. "We will manage somehow. I will go out every day to seek food. I will snare a creature, a monkey, whatever, if that's what it takes to keep you here."

Ithunzi had sighed. "You don't understand, Umia. The money

I will be able to send will help you and our parents survive the drought. You will be able to travel to the market, buy food, and if you want, share it with others. This is the only way I know to keep you and my baby from starving to death."

Finally, Umia had nodded submissively. He was right. It had been an awful year. The fields hadn't seen rain in months, and if the drought continued ... She didn't want to focus on that. They were young. They had plenty of time to be together when circumstance and time allowed.

Umia and Ithunzi shared a tearful farewell. Now, for the time being, Baby Ithunzi would have to fill the huge hole in Umia's heart caused by abandonment and loneliness.

After her delivery, Umia had little choice but to hear the latest gossip from those who came to her hut to offer congratulatory wishes. They said that Chief Naboto's daughter, Anele, was returning home today after an absence of thirty-three years. In different circumstances, Umia, like most other teenagers, would have been inquisitive. She would have asked, "Why did she leave? Was she sent away? Where did she go? Why is she coming back?" Instead, Umia's mind became consumed with her own question, "How am I going to cope as a single mother?" She wanted to lash out at the man who had fathered her child but was busy doing his "man thing."

When her hut emptied of guests, Umia swept the floor and thought back on how she had been so emotionally distraught recently. How she had begged her husband ... wailed for hours ... pleaded for him to stay ... beseeched him to be there after the birth of their first child. But her bright, educated husband had been emphatic when he concluded, "I want this child and my future children to have good lives. In order to accomplish this, I will find work in the diamond mines, save enough money to buy a *real* house in the city, and then come and get you and the child."

"In my heart of hearts, I don't want you to go, but yes, I love you for this sacrifice. Please come back soon," surrendered Umia.

"I promise, my love," Ithunzi replied.

Unforeseen circumstances would overrule that heartfelt pledge.

Umia was wrenched into the present by the sudden appearance of a child entering the hut and yelling at the new mother at the top of her lungs, "The chief wants you. You have to go to his hut, *now!*"

Umia's brows furrowed as she responded, "Why? What does he want?"

The little girl replied evasively, "Go quick, Umia, or else you'll be in big trouble."

"Fine," Umia huffed, "but I want you to stay here and mind my baby. Make sure the spiders don't bite him. If they do, I'll bite you."

The child's eyes, unblinking, widened like dinner plates. She flew to the crib, focused her vision on the sleeping baby, and stood as rigid as a sentry. Although Umia grinned outwardly at the girl's response, her inner thoughts were worried. She had never been summoned by Chief Naboto. Was she in trouble? Had word from her husband arrived? Had something bad happened to Ithunzi?

Fear of the unknown sprung Umia's legs into action, and as she neared Chief Naboto's hut, she saw him waving frantically for her to hurry up.

"You want to see me, Chief Naboto," she said in a trembling tone.

"Yes. Get inside, girl. My daughter needs help."

Naboto placed his hand on the small of Umia's back and literally shoved her inside. She let out a deep sigh of relief. There was no bad news.

Her apprehension dissipated as she approached the woman who was holding a swaddled crying baby in her arms. Before Umia could utter a word, Naboto announced to Anele, "You have your wet nurse." He poked Umia's shoulder. "Make my newborn grandchild healthy with your milk, girl." With that said, the chief of the village walked out of his hut.

From the light of several oil lamps, Umia was not surprised at what she saw. It was not uncommon for *older* women to give birth. And any one over twenty was *old* to this teenager.

Umia greeted Anele warmly. "Welcome home, daughter of Chief Naboto. My name is Umia. I have just given birth, too. I drink the milk of the goat to make sure my breasts are full." Cupping a hand under a swollen breast, she jiggled it up and down. "You should try it. I don't know the reason for your lack of milk flow, daughter of Naboto, but take my advice: Rich goat's milk does help."

Without waiting for a response, Umia plonked herself onto the dirt floor. Sitting cross-legged, she stretched forth her arms to receive Anele's baby. Anele was smiling. She warmed to this young girl, who didn't look old enough to bear a child. Anele, a former domestic servant, had forgotten that it was the norm here for girls as young as twelve to marry. A spark of envy dominated her thoughts. The girl's breasts were swollen like a milking cow, whereas her own first taste of motherhood, on the Hallworthy estate, had been completely different.

Anele sighed, bent, and handed the swaddled Shiya to Umia's waiting arms. When she received the baby, Umia's happy-to-be-of-help expression vanished in the blink of an eye. Umia's mouth opened wide. Her bloodcurdling cry shattered the still of the hut. With her screams bouncing off the mud walls like ping-pong balls, Umia sprang to her feet, sending baby Shiya flying across the floor. The child's piercing wails, and then Anele's shriek, joined the symphony of reverberating sounds.

Not far away, under the eaves of another hut, Naboto slumbered on the ground, oblivious to the mayhem occurring in his home.

Before the wet nurse had a chance to flee, Anele swept up her baby with one hand and fiercely latched on to Umia's arm with the other. "Umia, you *will* feed my baby!"

Umia shot Anele the evil eye. Wrapping her arms across her breasts, she snapped loudly, "*No!* I will never let the lips of an *umlungu* suckle at my breasts!"

That was back then. But that awful night in Naboto's hut had far from finished replaying itself. Umia buried her face in her hands as she was once more swept back in time.

Umia marched away from Anele and her white baby, went to her own hut, collected baby Ithunzi, and headed for the communal fire pit dining area, a meeting place where villagers relaxed after a long day's work, talked, and let off steam.

With her story of the white baby, the affronted teenager, with Ithunzi strapped to her back, brought the women's chattering to an abrupt halt. There was a lengthy silence before laughter pealed over the sounds of the crackling fire. An elderly woman stood up and said, "You have dung in your head, girl. There's no white baby here!"

Another woman added, "You better lay off the beer, girl, because it's pickling your brain."

Umia stomped her feet. "I'm not lying!" she protested defensively. "I've seen the baby. Go and see for yourselves. Are you all blind? Didn't you notice that the baby was *umlungu*? She's as white as the underbelly of a leopard."

A young boy, who had been down at the gate when Anele

arrived, pointed out a fact. "Chief Naboto's daughter didn't have a baby strapped to her back. She carried only a basket."

His statement sunk in. A tribeswoman who had also been in the proximity of the gate slapped her head. "She must have had that baby in the basket the whole time."

A little girl who sat quietly by her mother suddenly piped up. "Do you want me to go and see if Umia is telling the truth?"

"I wouldn't if I were you," another woman argued. "Chief Naboto's daughter could have you whipped for interfering in her business. Anyway, I think it's a lot of nonsense. I don't believe Umia. She never had a truthful tongue, even as a child."

Umia didn't bat an eyelid after that comment. She knew that they would learn the truth soon. And her argument was clear: She wanted the *stolen* white baby gone ... dead ... whatever ... but anywhere other than here in her home, Tswanas.

Tribal tongues wagged profusely back then and continued to do so for years to come.

As the elderly Umia emerged from her memories of 1945, fingers of sunlight shone through the only window in the tin-roofed shack and flickered over her as she sat in her chair. That past episode was fresh in her mind, but she could not endure any more of those memories. She rose from her chair with the intention of occupying her mind with more immediate matters, such as sweeping, washing clothes, or anything else that would stop the past from getting the better of her. She hardly made it to the broom closet when the power of recollection overcame her desire to forget.

Grudgingly, Umia gave way to the past, replaying the events that had taken place after the discovery of the baby's race. The reflection was troubling. She recalled how things had gotten out of control ... the fighting ... the verbal abuse ... the physical attack on

Anele ... and subsequently, her own banishment from the kraal, along with the departure of Kumdi and his family.

Naboto had died of a heart attack the day his daughter had returned to the village. It was then that another type of trouble began—a confrontation between Umia's brother, Kumdi, and Anele over a role Kumdi wanted to fill so badly, Chief of the village.

What caused Umia to cringe as she remembered those times in her broad-bottomed chair was an accusation made by her sister Vimbela.

"Kumdi made me lie down with him," Vimbela cried. "He's the father of my dead baby."

Life after that honest accusation could only be described as a living hell for those who had encountered the wrath of Anele's anger.

No matter how hard she tried, Umia couldn't block out those awful chapters of her life. Feeling that her mind was beaten and broken, she sank lower in her chair and allowed herself to be swept back to the merciless events that occurred after her departure from Tswanas Kraal.

CHAPTER NINE

The neighboring Zulu village of Mtunzini, the start of the New Year 1946

KUMDI—WITH HIS TWO PREGNANT WIVES, elderly parents, sister Umia, and her baby son in tow—left Tswanas for the neighboring village of Mtunzini, thirty miles away.

When the exhausted group arrived at Mtunzini, Kumdi told a pack of lies in order to gain sympathy from these tribespeople. After gasps and "ahs," the Mtunzini villagers condemned Chief Anele's banishment ruling and welcomed their homeless neighbors into their kraal to share their lives. That is, until two weeks later, when Umia's mouth got the better of her. Her loose tongue caused her family to outstay their welcome.

In the short period of time she was there, Umia was detested by the Mtunzini women, who, with justification, labelled the new mother as a lazy, good-for-nothing girl. Umia refused to help wet-nurse premature babies or help with other babysitting duties. And she flatly refused to work in the corn fields. Also, she declined to sleep with the chief, whose wives were past childbearing age.

The chief called a meeting, and before the moon rose in the heavens, it was communally agreed that the likes of Umia were no longer to be offered hospitality. The Mtunzini tribespeople had had enough of this troublesome girl. Her behavioral problems were not the norm in their culture. Unfortunately, her family was also affected by her conduct. They had to go, too.

Kumdi was furious when he learned of their new situation. He screamed at his sister, "Look what you've done! Where are we going to go now? How are we going to take care of our parents? How are we going to give our children food?" He continued to rage, "We have no money. We have nothing!"

"It's not my fault," Umia bemoaned. "It wasn't your wives who were asked to lie down with the ugly old chief! What would my husband have said?"

Kumdi shot Umia a murderous look and then marched off in the direction of the chief's hut. The only way to defuse the situation was to speak to him man to man.

On the way to see the chief, Kumdi made up his mind that he wasn't going to plead for Umia's life, but instead, for the lives of his wives and elderly parents.

"My mother and father are feeble with age," Kumdi told the chief. "I'm their sole provider. Please reconsider."

The chief placed a commiserating hand on Kumdi's shoulder, thinking that it wasn't his fault that things had turned out so badly. "I'm sorry, Kumdi," the chief said. "My hands are tied." He sighed and added heavily. "I will not tolerate being continuously badgered by my tribespeople to make all of you leave. My people have made their position clear: 'Make them go, or we go!'"

Kumdi, with his head lowered and his eyes blazing with anger, stormed out of the chief's hut.

The next day, well before sunrise, Kumdi snuck into the storage shed and stole enough food (dried meats and corn) for their journey. With his parents, wives, and children following him, Kumdi led the way out of the village.

Later that morning, Umia was awakened by shouts followed by hurtling stones. She snatched her baby from his makeshift crib and left behind what little possessions she owned. In fear of her life, she fled Mtunzini.

After walking at a fast pace for hours through thick brush and open plains, Umia flopped to the ground and began crying tears of regret. What had she done? Where could she go? Who was going to provide for her and her baby? Why was life so difficult?

When the new mother arrived back at Tswanas, the sun was setting fast. She entered the kraal and headed for the communal fire pit, where she begged for mercy. None came from the astonished villagers, but surprisingly, Anele was sympathetic. She gave Umia money, food, a machete (just in case), and a hand-drawn map showing her how to get to farming country near the city of Durban.

Anele informed Umia, "You must look for work—fieldwork, domestic work, or whatever can be found. Umia, you have little choice now but to try to build a new life for yourself and your infant son." Anele went on to stress that Umia must get a message to Tswanas once she was settled. It was imperative they let her husband know her whereabouts so he does not return to Tswanas and find her gone. In addition, Anele had a stark warning. "Listen carefully, Umia. Under no circumstances are you to deviate from the lines on the map I have drawn for you."

Anele knew that The Valley of a Thousand Hills route would have shortened Umia's journey by several days, but she could not bear the thought of this young girl unexpectedly stepping into the Devil's lair—the Hallworthy plantation—as she herself had done in 1928, many years ago. Was there work for Umia along the coastline? Anele didn't know. Umia had a baby. That would prevent her from getting a domestic job. Field work was Umia's only option. While it is backbreaking labor, mothers can work with their babies strapped to their backs.

Even though the two women had had their differences, Anele couldn't help extending her heart to the young mother. She lovingly wrapped her arms around Umia and said, "May the Gardener of all life on Earth protect you and keep you and your baby safe."

Umia's eyes filled with tears. "Forgive me, Chief Anele. I was not in my right mind."

"You are forgiven, child," Anele returned softly.

Umia felt a knot of fear tighten her stomach. "I'm scared, Anele," she cried. "Why can't I stay here? Please give me another chance? I was born here. This is my home. I know nothing of other ways. I don't speak any other languages. And I'm terrified of the *umlungu*. They might eat me and my baby."

Anele wanted to laugh, but she remembered how scared she had been when she had followed her twin sisters from this kraal. And yes, Umia had every right to be frightened. It was without a doubt an *umlungu*-dominated world, a world Anele never wanted to return to. If she never again saw a white man or woman again, she would go to her grave a happy tribeswoman.

Anele touched Umia's face, it was wet with tears. "I'm sorry Umia. I can't let you stay here. There would be rebellion if I did. You have burned your bridges, girl. It's time to move on. Go and make a new life for yourself and your son. I think you will be surprised how many white people can speak our native tongue …" Anele shuddered. She covered her mouth as she remembered how well Lord Alan Hallworthy had spoken her tongue. "I wish you well, Umia. I mean that from the bottom of my heart."

Umia heaved the longest sigh and let the tears fall.
Que sera sera.

CHAPTER TEN

Umia's journey into the unknown, 1946

WITH A SWARM OF PESKY FLIES accompanying her, Umia began her trek. Wearing a cotton skirt and loose-fitting top, she walked across a mountain range, scrambled down rugged cliffs, and trudged down paths trodden by wild animals. She stopped only to nurse her baby and find refuge up a tree at night. Yet she still did not see what Anele had described to her: a coastline with ocean water as high as mountains and homesteads as big as the sky. She was confused. Had she gone the wrong way? Even though she had not been able to read the words on the map, she had traced the map lines with her finger.

Eventually, she came across a field of tall sugar cane plants. She sighed with relief and headed toward the smoke that she saw belching from a chimney. How was she to know that she had just entered through the gates of hell?

As Umia neared the estate, she heard a welcome sound—

gushing water. Her throat was parched, so she let her ears guide her to the source. She found a fishpond with an ornate fountain in the center that spewed fresh water—sustenance from the heavens. Hastily, she scooped up handfuls of water. From the corner of her eye, she spotted big, bright yellow goldfish weaving in and out of the fountain's pond grasses. She had never seen fish this color. Could she catch one? Her last meal of dried corn kernels had been hours ago.

Umia removed her cotton skirt. It would make a good net, she thought. But to her dismay, the wary fish were so adapted to their habitat that they were able to effectively dart and hide from her drag-and-catch material. But Umia's improvised net did snatch an inflated toad. He was not happy to be scooped away from a large female he was trying to impress with his throaty songs. Umia grabbed it by its dark-patched feet, but instead of returning the creature to his domain, she flung it into a nearby bush.

After Umia dispatched the helpless amphibian, she found a flat rock to sit against so she could rest her aching back and breast-feed Ithunzi. At least he would not go hungry. Umia marvelled at how lucky she was. He had been such a good baby throughout the arduous journey. He had woken just to suckle and have his bottom changed. The he went straight back to sleep. After Umia drank half the fishpond water, she felt certain she could now produce plenty of milk. She looked up at the sky. It was darkening.

With her baby tucked and strapped securely into a "joey" pouch, Umia made her way toward the smoke plumes. The alley of oak trees leading to a large house cast eerie shadow fingers, an ominous sign, over the young mother from Tswanas. They seemed to be warning her to turn back. But how could she have known that the worst of evils lay ahead? Or that this very place was linked to fear ... by Anele and many other dark-skinned souls?

Umia, with wide eyes, was in awe of the impressive stone-carved sculptures that dotted the gardens. Everything was strange, yet these were wonderful sights. A few steps more and she couldn't believe her eyes. Ahead was the biggest building she had ever seen. Even though it looked intimidating, she took several deep breaths and made her way to the entrance.

Behind this picture-perfect setting lurked unspeakable darkness.

With one hand cupped under Ithunzi's behind, Umia rapped on the massive door with her free hand. As the door opened with gale force, she stepped back. Staring at her was a tall, blond man with a mean, hard look on his face. His steely blue eyes glared at her in a way that made her feel as if he could easily de-flesh her—devour her. Was her trepidation about being eaten by the *umlungu* about to become reality?

"You have some nerve knocking on my front door," Lord Hallworthy angrily snapped in English. "What do you want, *kaffir*?"

Fear rooted Umia's body to the spot. It took what seemed forever for her to find her voice. "*Umlungu* man, I'm looking for work and a place to stay."

"We don't hire *kaffir* mothers! Get the hell off my property," returned the forceful Zulu voice. His racial prejudice was obvious. She was just another *darkie*, unworthy of life.

The door slammed shut in Umia's face.

Even though the inexperienced bush girl wasn't practised at "reading" white people, her gut told her to *run, run, run*. However, exhaustion, hunger, and desperation overruled her sense of alarm. Umia plucked up her nerve and knocked on the door again. This time she wasn't put off by Lord Alan's balled fists. She straightened her back and said, "Please *Umlungu* man, the night is approaching fast. My legs are so weary. Isn't there somewhere my baby and I could rest for the night? I'll be gone before the cock crows. If you change your mind, I'll work from dawn to dusk. And if you can spare me some food, I'll be fit for work by tomorrow."

Alan stepped closer. Umia stepped back. Her head was bowed; nevertheless, she felt his beady eyes pierce right through her, checking out every inch of her wholesome frame. It wasn't compassion that caused this criminal mastermind to nod and reply in her native tongue, "Okay. I'm feeling charitable today. I'll find something for you. But get this, *kaffir*. You will address me as Master Hallworthy. Got that?"

Umia nodded. She was surprised to note how well he spoke Zulu. It was just what Anele had pointed out when she said, "It sounds crazy, but a lot of white folk speak our tongue." Why he had not done so from the beginning was a mystery. If she had guessed that this man—who had no conscience, not a scintilla of remorse, zero empathy—had caused the death of Anele's twin sisters as well as the demise of many other souls, Umia would have had second thoughts. *If it is too good to be true, it probably is.*

For sure, Umia didn't like the looks of the man, but she was famished and tired, and her baby needed changing. His bowel movement was seeping through the wraparound cotton material.

With a wave of dismissal, Lord Alan said, "Go back the way you came and wait at the end of the garden. I'll send someone to see to you. Thank your lucky stars, girl, that I'm giving you this chance to prove yourself to me."

The plan behind those diabolical words could be described as living hell. But Umia didn't know that yet.

Umia had no idea how long she had been waiting at the appointed spot, but finally she was relieved to see a young black girl whose arms were wrapped around her chest as she approached.

Maekela, one of Alan Hallworthy's many half-caste offspring, didn't want to obey his orders: "Take her to the cottage (the infamous abode where many unsuspecting spirits had been crushed), and give her food." Although she hesitated, if Alan, a beast, did not find this unsuspecting girl in the cottage when he came in later that night, Maekela's head would be on the chopping block. She knew she was expendable, just like the rest of the Hallworthy slaves.

From inches away, Maekela noted Umia's full figure. She was not that attractive, but the fresh-faced girl with a Mona Lisa smile was the right age for Alan's perversions. Maekela's conscience gave her a nudge. Should she or shouldn't she follow Alan's orders?

Maekela's conscience spoke to her powerfully. She grabbed Umia hand. "Go. Get away from here. Take your child and run like a cheetah before it is too late. This place belongs to the Dark One from the underworld. He is so evil that you and your child are in mortal danger."

Umia stared at Maekela as if she had two heads.

"I don't understand," Umia uttered.

Maekela shrugged. She didn't have the luxury of time to get her dire message through to the girl. "Quickly, come with me," Maekela said. "I'll hide you until morning. Then you *must* leave. Don't ever come back here."

"Hide me! Why should I hide?" Umia argued. "The *umlungu* man has offered me work. I need the work. How else will I feed myself and my baby?"

Maekela sighed heavily and pondered, "Would I choose the more favorable option of starving to death or this alternative— being worn down and murdered by Alan's sickness?" She couldn't truly answer because up to now both she and her sister had been spared their master's debauchery. Obviously, their young mother had not!

If Maekela had only known that this girl just recently had been with Anele, the person she loved and missed the most, she immediately would have escorted Umia off the estate, regardless of consequences.

There wasn't a day that went by that Maekela and her younger sister, Isona, did not shed tears for the sudden disappearance of their adopted mother. They longed for her. Life was so empty without their substitute mother. Was she dead? Killed by her heartless Hallworthy owners? Had she joined her twin sisters in the Invisible Kingdom? If not, was she happy? But of course, why wouldn't she be happy? She was free of this horrible place.

Early the next morning, on Lord Alan's instructions, Maekela reluctantly went to the guest cottage to let Umia out and take her to the farm overseer, who would set her to work in the fields. When she entered the infamous cottage, her heart hit the floor. She wanted to cry when she witnessed Lord Hallworthy's handiwork. Umia's left eye was so swollen that Maekela couldn't tell if an eye socket ever existed there. Umia's arms had fresh bruising, the telltale markings of restraints, and her swollen upper lip was caked with blood.

Umia sprang up from the floor, lunged at the Hallworthy servant, and latched onto her wrist screaming hysterically, "You brought me here. You knew what was going to happen to me, and you did nothing about it! I have been violated! My husband won't look at me now!" Fresh blood splayed from gums that were missing two teeth. "I pleaded for my life, but he wouldn't listen. He took my baby. Where's my baby? What has the *umlungu* devil done with my son? Has he eaten little Ithunzi?"

Umia fell to her knees, let out a cry, then covered her mouth and let the tears fall. Turning her head heavenward, she prayed, "God of the Invisible Kingdom, protect my mother's heart from breaking in two. Return my son from the mouth of the *umlungu* crocodile." She began beating her chest with the full force of her fists.

Maekela, the indentured kitchen worker who had placed a thumbprint marking that legally bound her to servitude, didn't truly understand the ways of primitive bush people. She had been born on the Hallworthy estate. What she wanted to say was, "I warned you, but you didn't listen." But Maekela couldn't bring herself to make this girl feel more wretched than she already did.

"I want my baby," Umia cried. "Where's my baby?"

Maekela didn't have the answer, but nothing surprised her anymore in this godforsaken place. "Come, Umia," she said extending her hand. "You must come with me. I'll take you to the servant quarters. I have some clean clothes for you, and then you have to start work."

Losing her mind, Umia's fists beat the peeling wallpaper. "I will *never* work a minute for the *umlungu*. For the love of me, I can't go on! I want to die. The *umlungu* man has defiled my womanhood and eaten my baby. I have nothing to live for any more."

Maekela felt her heart wrenching from her body. She wrapped her arms around the shaking girl, comforting her as best she could. "You mustn't think like that. Death is what awaits this demon man. Death does not await you. Think of your baby. He is probably being looked after by another worker." Maekela looked at her feet so as not to be caught in a lie. "He is okay." She knew that no baby, black or white, was safe from Alan's evil ways.

Most babies were sold and became servants of other white folk. Slavery, even though it was abolished by law, was still very much alive on this impregnable, above-the-law estate. Throughout the continent, human trafficking was still rampant. "Has this happened to Umia's child?" Maekela wondered. In order to save this poor bush girl's life, Maekela bluffed, "Come. Let's go and find your baby. I know where he could be."

The ploy worked.

Maekela's strong arms supported the crestfallen Umia as they walked from the guest cottage toward a shack that Maekela shared with her sister, Isona, and the manor cook, Lamella. Lamella had been employed at Hallworthy Manor long before the orphaned sisters were born. Oh, how Cook kept them spellbound with her tales.

But this particular night, it was past eleven o'clock when Lamella entered the dilapidated quarters she had called home for more years than she could count. She took one look at the battered, sobbing Umia—who had been hidden in the shack during daylight hours—and put a hand over her heart. It was déjà vu. Even though her brain was fighting reality, Lamella let her mind wander back in time.

It all began in the summer of 1927 when another young African bush girl sat in this very spot bawling her eyes out. And just like Umia, a young Anele had also accidentally stumbled onto this estate and subsequently become a victim of this white man's despicable and unforgiving lust. Only a few years later, *her* child had been taken from her and handed over to the renegade priest, Father Batuzi.

And now, seeing Alan's latest victim in such despair, Lamella had a gut-wrenching feeling that Umia would not see her child again, dead or alive.

As it happens, Cook was wrong.

Lamella let her tears fall. She, like her kitchen assistants, Maekela and Isona, missed and loved Anele who was the daughter Lamella never had. One dark evening, they had been separated … by force. How could Lamella ever forget the ghastly night a powerful hand had clamped over her mouth? She closed her eyes, stepped back in time, and saw herself being forcefully restrained by a giant of a man. "Be quiet, Lamella," Alan ordered that dark night. "You are coming with me."

The first thought that entered Cook's mind back then was "I'm too old for him! And a person doesn't need to just accept things. One should ask why."

But the unspoken words failed to come to the fore.

Lamella did as she was ordered. She slipped quietly from the bed that she shared with Anele, who was snoring loudly, oblivious to what was happening.

With Alan's hand firmly gripping her bare shoulder, Lamella, wearing a flimsy hand-me-down petticoat she used as a nightgown, exited the hut. She shivered in the late night air. There was a chill in her voice when she finally plucked up the courage to ask, "Master, where are you taking me?"

"You will soon find out," Lord Alan fired back. "Hurry up and get in there."

Lamella tucked her petticoat between her legs and climbed into the trunk of Alan's vehicle. As they sped off in high gear, she was tossed about like a leaf in a windstorm. If she had been twenty years old, she would have forced open the trunk and dived out of the contraption in mid-flight.

Alan brought the car to a screeching halt on the manor's circular driveway. Waiting for him on the doorstep was his wife, Lady Corrie. Wearing a candlewick bathrobe and fluffy pink slippers, she made her way to the back of the vehicle. Careful not to break a manicured, polished fingernail, she lifted the trunk door, exposing her servant, whose breathing was irregular with fear.

Corrie announced, "Lamella, as of today, you will be working for another family ... and I'm warning you. If I get wind of you breathing a word to your new mistress or to any of her staff about private happenings here at Hallworthy Manor, you will vanish off the face of the Earth. Do you hear me?"

A visibly shaken Lamella bobbed her head, wondering what was going on. If she was only going to work for another household, why was she being taken this way? Couldn't she have been told about it when she came to work in the morning? Something wasn't right, but poor Cook couldn't put two and two together.

Lady Corrie slammed the trunk shut, said goodbye to her husband, and returned indoors. "She's just an ape. I'm not upset about it," she muttered. "There are plenty more where she came from." But her outburst was far from the truth. Lamella was the best chef a household could have, and Corrie knew she would only be able to get an inexperienced replacement.

Lying in total darkness, Lamella never imagined that *she* had been the final *stake* at a poker game. Alan had gambled thousands of pounds and lost. Unable to meet the hefty tab without having to ask his wife for the money, he took a chance and placed his prized cook, well renowned for her culinary skills, into the pot. The winner, Steven James Smith, a rising politician, immediately accepted the unusual bid. His wife, Jane, had been jealous of Lady Corrie's cook for some time and had often asked Corrie to part with her. Corrie's response had always been *"Never."*

Steven Smith thought his wife could get even with Corrie, a woman she had detested from the very first time they'd met. That Hallworthy aristocrat was, to say the least, arrogant, rude, and uncouth. However, her husband, Alan, was even worse. He was only tolerated by the Smiths because of his influence and more-than-generous donation to Steve's election campaign. Alan had hundreds of contacts, moneyed men who bowed down to him—a man who was distantly related to Queen Victoria.

In the fall of 1932 Alan had returned home from that poker game and confessed his wager. Corrie became hysterical. She threw an ashtray at him, and he ducked.

"You imbecile!" she growled. "Where am I going to find another cook like Lamella? How much did you lose? I'll gladly give Steven Smith his money. But he's not going to have my cook."

An hour after the car carrying Lamella had left the Hallworthy estate, Anele awoke to find her bed partner missing. Anele naturally assumed the cook had decided to go to work earlier than usual.

When Anele entered the kitchen at her usual time, she expected to find Lamella already hard at work. But instead, Corrie was standing there with her hands on her hips.

"Where's Lamella?" the eighteen-year-old servant asked.

Lady Corrie, whose night attire had been replaced with a brown, V-neck frock, snappily said, "Anele, you are late. Don't let this happen again." She thrust the week's menu instructions at the bewildered girl, who had been working as Lamella's kitchen helper. "I've no choice but to make you the cook now."

"I don't understand, Mistress? Where is Lamella? Has something happened to her?"

"She's gone, Anele," Corrie said nastily. "That's all you need to know. Now get to work."

Anele bowed her head. What else could she do? According to the man who built Hallworthy manor, she was nothing more than an ape!

Even though she felt her heart had been ripped from her chest, Anele got on with her lot. She slaved away for thirteen years until she found an opportunity to escape the enforced domestic captivity. The opportunity arose on Christmas Day 1945.

Anele's escape and what was in store for her afterward would change her life, and the lives of many other people, forever.

Would Umia follow in her footsteps and escape this hellish place?

Not yet.

Trapped by circumstance, Umia worked herself to the bone in unbearable temperatures. She cut sugar cane in the fields from sunup to long past sundown. But it was after nightfall that her life worsened. The infamous cottage became her after-hours work.

Ithunzi, her now two-year-old son, cried pitifully outside the door while Lord Hallworthy did his thing. The child had been the ransom: "You please me, and you can keep your son."

Then one day, Umia overheard a conversation about a former servant and a foreigner. She couldn't believe her ears. It took a while to sink in that this place was the same imprisonment Anele of Tswanas had escaped from with a foreign, pregnant girl who also had been held as a sex-slave in the infamous cottage. There were loud gasps when Umia told Maekela and Isona that Anele was alive in Tswanas and that she had come home with an *umlungu* child. But Umia insisted that she knew nothing of the whereabouts of the girl named Maria, who had not accompanied Anele to Tswanas.

It didn't take long for Maekela to put two and two together. "May the Gardeners of all Life protect Anele and the child of Maria, named Shiya."

One fall morning in 1949 (a year before the abduction of Shiya from Tswanas), Umia, age nineteen, was summoned from fieldwork by Lord Alan. He ordered brusquely, "Go to the house and see my wife. She needs another kitchen helper." He gave her a stern look. "You are to go to the back door and knock." Oh, how Umia remembered the cold, spine-shivering reception she had received when she dared to knock on the *front* door of this white man's castle. But would she have a warm reception at the *back* door? She didn't ponder that for long.

Umia grabbed her four-year-old son, who was sleeping under a horse buggy, and ran to the manor house as if her life depended on it.

In the years that followed, Lady Corrie's latest kitchen slave could be heard singing African tunes while she peeled mountains of potatoes. By now she had accepted her lot and had left behind her personal war of regret at coming to this place. She didn't have any choice but to integrate herself into this white world. How else was she to house and feed herself and her son in the aftermath of WWII? Every day, black and white migrants were turning up looking for work, and they were sent away hungry and dejected. Yes, she counted herself lucky to have work, even if it was under a dark veil of ugliness.

· One afternoon, when Umia was rinsing dirt from the spuds, she happened to look out the scullery window. A dark stranger was heading toward the basement kitchen. Umia didn't recognize her husband. He was gaunt and dull eyed, and his hair was white as snow.

"Umia, can you come here?" Maekela called out. "Someone is asking for you."

Umia wiped her wet hands on her apron and headed for the back door. She checked out the man and still was no wiser. "Who are you? What do you want?"

"Umia, my wife, I have at last found you."

Umia felt her knees buckle. "It can't be you!" she cried. "How did you find me?"

Ithunzi cupped Umia's face in his hands. "I returned to the kraal and was told that you had been gone twelve years," he answered. "And I have been travelling from farm to farm since I heard that news in the hopes of finding you at last."

Umia flung her arms around her husband's skeletal frame. Winded by her remarkable strength, he coughed and spluttered. Then, mustering his own strength, he gently untangled her arms. "It's good to see you, my wife, but I need food and water."

Umia grabbed a pitcher of freshly squeezed orange juice and a fresh loaf of bread. She cared not at all that these delights were meant solely for her employers. No, she would steal any amount of food to satisfy her husband's needs. She watched in disbelief as Ithunzi Senior put the pitcher to his mouth and gulped continuously until the jug was emptied. Next, he bit into the bread, swallowing whole chunks at one time. Umia clasped her hand over her mouth and watched in alarm as his stomach rebelled and the acid contents of undigested food hurtled over her bare feet and kitchen floor. When he straightened, she touched his sunken cheek. "Oh, my dear husband, I can't bear to see you so ill. Come. I will take you to the servant quarters where you can rest up and I can take care of you ..."

Suddenly a formidable presence entered the kitchen and cut Umia's intentions short.

"Who's this *kaffir*?" Lady Corrie demanded. "What business has he here and in *my* kitchen?"

"He's my husband, Mistress Corrie. He's sick. Is it all right to take him to ..." She paused so as not to give away her true purpose "... the old unused barn at the back of the gardens so he can rest?"

Lady Corrie's upper lip curled into a snarl. "Absolutely not!" she barked. "You should know by now that black men aren't allowed on my property without permission!" She strode to the pair, poked the sickly Ithunzi in the ribs with her walking cane, and threatened, "Get out of this kitchen. Go from my property now or I will send for my husband. He won't be as nice." Turning her attention to Umia, she added, "Get back to work."

Defiantly and wordlessly, Umia threw her apron on the floor, latched onto her husband's forearm, and left through the main kitchen door. She did not look back. "Ithunzi, come quick," she yelled at her son, who was kicking a football near the fishpond. He rushed to his mother's side and stared at the man his mother was holding up. Umia took the boy's hand and placed it in Ithunzi Senior's. "This is your father, child. He is sick. I'm taking him and you somewhere safe away from here."

Unquestioning, the boy nodded in agreement.

Umia's shoulders were hurting from all but carrying her husband to the outskirts of the Hallworthy estate. When Ithunzi Senior protested that his legs could walk no more, Umia found a shady spot under a tree, lowered him to the ground, and kissed him on the lips. Within seconds he was deep in slumber ... but not for long.

The dust trail from the approaching vehicle could be seen for miles. Umia screamed to her son. "Hurry, child. Do as you are told. Climb that tree and hide yourself."

Satisfied that her son was not visible, she ran toward the oncoming truck in an effort to distract the driver from seeing her loved ones. Umia closed her eyes and waited for the crash that would end her life. She believed that being run over was an unselfish and preferable choice to the cruelty that her husband and son would endure if they were found. She didn't stop to reason how a twelve-year-old could take care of his dying father.

A shower of arid earth sprayed Umia from head to toe. She braced herself for impact, but the truck's bumper stopped within inches of her stiffened body.

Alan, his eyes blazing like hot coals, appeared as a rabid animal. "You are a dead bitch!" he spat, levelling a rifle. "Give me one good reason why I shouldn't shoot you."

The plain-speaking Tswanas maiden-of-old returned with a brazen retort: "Kill me if you want. I don't care. I'm already dead because of you. You murdered me when you took from me what wasn't yours to take."

Alan chortled. He looked at her as if she were nothing more than feces stuck to his boot and gloated. "You are going to die without my bullet. From what I'm told, your husband has AIDS, and you *kaffirs* can't get enough sex, so why waste a bullet?"

Umia was ignorant of the fact that this deadly virus was spreading throughout Africa and that one day she also would be a victim of its destructive wrath.

"You have a half hour to get off my property," Alan said. "If I find you here after that, you are dead ... all of you."

Two days later, a grieving Umia buried her husband in a deserted cornfield in the Valley of a Thousand Hills. It was the very same ground where the two unwanted newborns had been interred years ago. As it happened, Shiya's life had been miraculously saved, but her twin sister's remains had long ago been disseminated by animals.

After spending a lengthy time at her husband's burial site, Umia, with Anele's map in her pocket, headed for the only place she knew—her birthplace. She did not know if she or her son would be welcomed or ousted again. But it was a risk she was prepared to take.

It came to pass that a virus-free Umia remained in Tswanas until 1993, when her grown-up son, Ithunzi Junior, came for her and brought her to his marital home in Soweto. It was in her son's house that she contracted the deadly virus—from Ithunzi's wife, Dora. While her son was working in a gold mine, Umia kept house. She fed and bathed her pregnant daughter-in-law. After Umia had cut herself with a sharp knife, Dora's infected blood found its way into Umia's veins.

Dora died shortly after giving birth to Amalonda, who carried her mother's disease.

A few months later, Ithunzi Junior died in a gold mine fatality.

With Umia close to death, Amalonda was often left in the care of her drunken relatives.

But not for long. An unexpected savior would turn up and rescue the six-year-old girl from a life of neglect.

CHAPTER ELEVEN

Back at the Tswanas burial ground, Monday, December 14, 2009

WHILE SEATED ON THE EXCAVATOR'S bucket seat, Mandegizi reached for his jacket and removed his radio phone. A pleased smile creased his dark face when he heard a weak voice crackling through the distortion: "Hello. This is Mrs. Umdaba."

"Mother, it is Mandegizi. I need you to do something for me."

"How wonderful it is to hear from you," Nellie Umdaba exclaimed. "When are you coming home?"

"Not for a while, Mother. But listen. I don't have many minutes left on my phone, and I don't know when it's going to cut out, so I will speak quickly. I want you to find a nun ..."

"Did I hear right? You want me to find a nun?"

"Please, Mother, don't interrupt. Her name is Sister Bertha. I think she's running a school in Soweto. If you find her, tell her I need her help with one of the tribespeople left behind at Tswanas. On second thought, go to the Catholic Church behind our house and ask the priest if he can get hold of her. Call me back as soon as you have made contact. Okay?"

"I will do what I can. I love you."

"I love you, too, Mother." He hung up the phone and tucked it into his shirt pocket. Then he grabbed his jacket, got out of the excavator, and headed back to Vimbela, who was lying prone in the dirt. He bent down and covered her naked body with his coat. She didn't stir. He spoke to her back: "Vimbela of the Ancients, I'm a good man and can't bear to see you like this. Please let me help you."

No response.

"I'm waiting for a call from Sister Bertha, whom I'm sure you know. As soon as she contacts me, we will get you away from here."

No response.

Mandegizi sighed. "You must be thirsty and hungry. I have a sandwich and some coffee. Would you like some?"

No response.

A feeling of doom raced through the machine operator's body. He fell to his knees and lifted the woman's dirt-caked head. Vimbela's dull, dead eyes stared vacantly into his. With his adrenalin pumping, Mandegizi pressed his index finger on a vein in her neck. No pulse. He tried her wrist. Nothing. He then placed his hand on her heart. Again, nothing. Mandegizi's body went limp. He felt dread pinch his stomach. A rush of tears flowed down his cheeks as he cried, "No, no, no, spirited woman. You can't be dead! Only minutes ago, you were breathing the fire of existence. Why did you give up so easily?"

Mandegizi lit a cigarette. His head screamed "Now what?" as he remembered Vimbela's plea to "Bury me with my ancestors." But how could he? His orders were to eliminate the site.

A sudden dose of fear sent Mandegizi's arms and legs rushing away from Vimbela's dead body. His eyes searched for a weapon, a stick, anything at hand to kill the deadly black mamba that was slithering out from under the old woman's body ... and heading toward him. Beads of sweat rolled down his temples. Much to his relief, the snake stopped its forward motion. It flicked its tongue, stared into his eyes, and took a detour into thick, long-fingered bushes. Had this feared creature of the African bush caused Vimbela's demise?

Mandegizi gently turned Vimbela over. To the naked eye, there were no visible signs of bloody puncture marks that would have suggested death from a poisonous bite. But he was baffled by what he did see. Several eagle feathers were stuck to the flesh of her abdomen. How did they get there? They certainly were not visible earlier when she had risen to confront him.

Roused by Vimbela's death, Mandegizi worked tirelessly and without a break until sundown. The clunking sound of a metal bucket hitting and digging up the earth permeated the dry air on the grassy knoll. Vimbela and all her ancestors were now interred along the fence line in an oblong trench—six feet deep and a hundred yards in length.

With an inward shrug, Mandegizi thought silently, "Life is precious beyond price. I've now done my best to honor them in death."

As the full moon rose after the job was done, Mandegizi drove his machine back to the work yard. It was past ten o'clock when his radio phone beeped an incoming signal.

"Hello. Mandegizi Umdaba speaking."

"Hello, Mr. Umdaba," Sister Bertha greeted. "I hope it's not too late, but your mother told me to call you. She said it was urgent."

With a soft voice, Mandegizi broke the news to Bertha of

Vimbela's death. He heard her gasp and say in a shocked and grieving voice, "Why did you wait so long to call me?"

Mandegizi didn't have the answer, but he did tell her what he had done with Vimbela's body. He begged her to remain silent about the relocated interment. He told Bertha that he wanted to give her Vimbela's beaded ankle bracelets, which he'd removed before her burial. "Maybe you could bury them in hallowed ground?"

"Yes, I will do that," Bertha's replied.

"Goodbye, Sister. I will see you soon."

Bertha sat in the church vestry and wept. It was the worst phone call she had ever received. It was a shattering psychological blow. People often look back and wonder what they could have done differently in a particular situation. Could Vimbela's death have been prevented? Had Mandegizi really not seen a snake's bite marks on Vimbela's body?

Bertha had lived long enough with the Tswanas tribe to know that snakes were revered. According to the tribe's superstitious beliefs, snakes were messengers—guardians of life, death, fate, and destiny. They also represented the rod of temptation. Hadn't a serpent been depicted in the *Bible*? Bertha had not closed her mind to tribal beliefs and unexplained happenings. She wondered why these dangerous creatures had not killed little Shiya years ago? Shiya played with mambas like a modern child plays with dolls.

These revered creatures were always present at funerals. Bertha thought back to the day of Anele's funeral. A snake appeared then, too. Shiya had picked it up and placed the "guardian" on Anele's coffin, to accompany her into the afterlife.

Sister Bertha did not sleep easily that night. She dwelled on the fact that she had let Vimbela down. How could she live with herself? She had not kept her promise to go back, collect the simple woman, and bring her safely to Soweto. Her despair boiled down to this: *The root of all evil ...* money. The South African government would never be held accountable for the greedy economics that had destroyed human life. Indirectly, they had murdered Vimbela.

The tribe's relocation funds were long gone, depleted the day after she had arrived with the displaced tribespeople. Every day after that, Bertha *had* struggled with her conscience. She had prayed every day for a miracle. No money had ever appeared, though, for her to retrieve Vimbela. Now the grieving nun's mind was made up. She had to let go of the anger and pain if she was to move forward. Vimbela's life-and-death struggle would forever remain in the nun's heart, as well as in the heart of the machine operator. Vimbela would not be forgotten. Bertha wanted to believe that the simple-minded woman was in a better place.

Wrong!

Vimbela would remain earthbound until what belonged to her was returned to her.

CHAPTER TWELVE

Tuesday, December 15, 2009, Amalonda's revelation

UMIA'S GRANDDAUGHTER, AMALONDA, was full of beans. Not literally, of course, but with excitement. It was unmistakeable. The thought of sucking on a lollipop propelled her at springbok speed to run up the road toward the school. All she could think about since rising that morning was strawberry candy, her preferred flavor. But then any flavor was better than none. If she was fast enough to be the first child seated in the front row, she would get the first pick. That was the rule.

Amalonda was way ahead of the other kids when, suddenly, her legs stopped and set in place as if they were stuck in cement. Why couldn't she move? Why were her legs glued to one spot? Why did she feel as if someone was watching her? Then she saw her.

Amalonda squinted at the tall, slender woman directly in front of her. Mesmerized, the child stared at a woman who was clad in a floor-length, white-satin, princess-style wedding dress that was decorated with thousands of tiny pearls. The figure was topped with a crown of white roses and a white tulle veil. Amalonda was bedazzled; she continued to fix her eyes on the ethereal vision. Could it be? Was it really *she*?

Unaware that the other children, who were passing her by, were pointing and snickering at her as she kneeled, Amalonda spoke to the gossamer figure. "Who are you? What do you want?"

"I want you to give your grandmother, Umia, a message."

"You can give it to her yourself. She lives down there," Amalonda said pointing behind her. "I'm going to be late for school." Funny, Amalonda thought. Why hadn't the other children stopped, like she did, to stare at this strange white woman dangling in the air?

The spectre's voice was soft. "No, child, I don't want to alarm your grandmother. *You* have to tell her my secret."

With her brows raised in wonder, Amalonda bobbed her head. "What secret is that?"

"Come closer so you don't miss a word. Your grandmother's life and your life depend on it."

Ten minutes later, an adrenalin-motivated, out of breath six-year-old burst through the school's front door. Her words gushed out like a bursting dam. "Sister, Sister, I saw the Virgin Mary! She spoke to me. My hand disappeared through hers."

Sitting at her teacher's desk, Sister Bertha "tut-tutted" and said, "You are late, Amalonda."

Raucous laughter from the other children brought instant disapproval from the teacher. "Quiet!" Bertha ordered the classroom. "Begin the spelling assignment. If I hear another sound out of you, none of you will be given a candy treat. Do you hear me?"

Heads snapped downward, followed by silence. Bertha commanded Amalonda, "Go to the side room and wait for me. I will be with you shortly."

Bertha didn't take her eyes off Amalonda, who, with her head lowered, proceeded to the school's supply room. Sister Bertha watched her go. She was well aware of this particular child's imagination. Amalonda loved to make up stories. There had been the lioness that, supposedly, had snuck into Umia's home late one night and taken the girl's corn-dolly. Then there was a *white* man who had laid a stack of sugar cane next to her bed. Next came a dark man who said he was her Uncle Kumdi and that he would protect her from evil. However, Sister knew that Kumdi, the wannabe Tswanas chief, was long dead—shot in the head in 1950. But the tall tale Amalonda was now spinning had a totally different ring to it. The vision of Bernadette Soubirous kneeling in the grotto at Lourdes flashed into Sister Berta's mind. She quickly dismissed *that* image.

Bertha entered the supply room and found Amalonda trembling as she stood rigidly against the whitewashed dividing wall. "Am I in trouble? What have I done wrong?" she wailed.

"Calm down. Calm down," Bertha soothed. The Sister took hold of Amalonda's cold hand and led her to an old chair that was sitting in the corner. "Sit down, child, and tell me the truth. What is it that makes you shake like tall grass in a windstorm?"

Amalonda squirmed on the hard seat and said defensively, "I'm not crazy! I know she was real. The lady knew my name. She knew my grandma's name. She knew your name. She was floating in the air. She wore a white dress ..." Amalonda gulped air. "The Virgin Mary told me that we could all be rich if we listened to what she had to say. She said she will lead you to the place where she buried her jewelry. It's under a tree. And she told me to tell you that she is grateful to you and Zepsiweli for saving her life ..."

Bertha's hand flew over the child's mouth, and Amalonda's deluge of words came to an abrupt stop. In breathless silence, Bertha tried to make sense of the ramblings that threatened her own sanity. How could this be? Amalonda could not have known that in August of 1998 she had, indeed, taken the nine-year-old Tswanas boy, Zepsiweli, with her as she hastened to alert the game warden.

Bertha released her grip over the child's mouth. She cupped her hand under Amalonda's tearful face and raised it to eye level. "How do you know this, child?"

Amalonda crossed and re-crossed her legs. She stared for a long time before answering. "The white lady, the Virgin Mary, she told me. She said you and the boy travelled on mules from the same kraal where my grandma was born in order to get help—to stop her from bleeding to death. That's what she said. And she also told me that she wished she had accepted the silver cross you once offered her. It might have saved her."

The nun's eyes fixed sternly onto Amalonda's round face, giving her a moment to take in what her mind did not comprehend. Nothing was making sense. Could a split-reality delusion be the side effect of the antiviral drug Amalonda was receiving?

Bertha finally processed the fact that this little girl could not have known anything about the 1998 events. She hadn't yet been born. But there was doubt. Could Zepsiweli, who worked as a janitor at this school, have told Amalonda theses facts? Bertha brushed that thought away. Zepsiweli had no contact with the children during school hours. He cleaned the premises at night. And he lived on the other side of the township, nowhere near Amalonda's home.

Amalonda filled the silence by grabbing Sister Bertha's hand

and crying. "I know you don't believe me, but it's true. The Virgin Mary's real name is Shiya, the Forsaken One. Sh*ee*-I-ya. Sh*ee*-I-ya," she repeated phonetically.

Bertha's legs began to shake and her hands began to sweat. She rushed out of the supply room and into the classroom muttering, "It's impossible. This is not happening. It's a trick of the devil. Yes. It is Satan who is invading my sanity. Our Father who art ..."

Tittering could be heard behind her back. The classroom of students had been all ears. Their high-pitched chattering sounded like tin cans falling down stairs. Sister Claudia was not amused. To bring the students to order, she rapped the chalkboard with a ruler. "That's enough!" she demanded. "Not another sound or this ruler will find your knuckles."

Claudia looked at her superior and gasped. Bertha was holding Amalonda by the scruff of her neck. "Be gone, Satan, from this child," Bertha loudly demanded. "You are not going to use this child as an instrument to trick me."

Although alarmed by Bertha's outburst and Amalonda's distressed shrieks, Claudia prudently decided it was not her place to intervene. After all, she had to obey and respect her mentor. She directed her attention to the visibly frightened school children and said, "Kneel by your desks and let us pray ..."

Aware that all eyes were focused on her, Bertha took Amalonda to her quarters behind the schoolhouse. Out of ears' reach, and believing that she could get through to the possessed child before it was too late, Bertha spoke softly: "Forgive me, Amalonda. I didn't mean to be so rough, but I need you to be truthful. Okay?" She hesitated as if to catch a lie. "You know that God punishes the wicked, especially those who tell untruthful stories. Now tell me, where did you get the name 'Shiya'? Was it from your grandmother?"

Amalonda appeared sad faced. Tears rolled down her cheeks. She protested. "I am telling the truth, Sister. I swear to God. The lady said you wouldn't believe me. But she said you will change your mind when I tell you that her special name is Shiya." As if in a trance, Amalonda's soft voice sounded like a recording. "And that you and her were friends. And you came to see her in a white people's hospital when she had a bullet in her head."

As the gravity of the moment hit home, Sister Bertha's jaw set. She dropped to her knees and clasped her hands in prayer. Trying to keep a tight lid on her fragile mental state, she gripped the silver cross strung around her neck so tightly that it cut into her flesh.

Amalonda stared numbly at her teacher's bowed head. But it was the steady flow of blood trickling from the nun's index finger that motivated Amalonda. She ran out of the room yelling, "Sister Claudia. Come quick. Sister Bertha is dying."

If a dark-skinned person could turn *white*, the kneeling nun just proved it. Bertha glanced at her feet. There, poking out of her long tunic was a pair of well-worn, frequently mended Italian sandals given to her by the very person Amalonda mentioned.

"Sister, what's going on?" a bewildered Claudia asked. "Are you all right? Your finger is bleeding. Would you like me to get a Band-Aid?"

"Oh, it's nothing, Sister," Bertha replied, rising to her feet. She made a resolute face and reprimanded herself silently: "Get hold of yourself, woman. This is not real. Besides, you don't believe in ghosts." She instructed Sister Claudia, "Go back to the classroom and see to the children. I will be along in a minute." Bertha called out to the child hiding behind Sister Claudia. "Come here, Amalonda. Don't be scared. I need to speak to you."

As soon as Sister Claudia's back was turned, Bertha lost control of her placid demeanor and forced the child down onto the cot bed. "What rubbish!" Bertha said in a flat voice. "Tell me the truth. Did your grandmother make up this story for you to tell me?"

Amalonda shook under the nun's fierce grip. "No, no, Sister Bertha," she protested. "It's true. The lady even told me that she was pleased that you never threw away the sandals she gave you, and ..."

Bertha's loud exhalation ended the girl's speech.

Amalonda gaped at Bertha, whose eyes were as large as the oval stool standing nearby. The bedroom door opened. Sister Claudia's reappearance halted the tension in the bedroom. "I'm sorry to intrude, Sister. But I'm concerned. Is everything all right? Can I be of help?"

Bertha looked at her kind novice and decided that she was too young and sensitive to understand. So she said, "Everything is fine, Sister Claudia. But please take over my class."

"Of course. Without question," Claudia replied.

Seconds after Claudia's departure, Sister Bertha looked at the long-faced child in front of her. Bertha wanted to wrap her arms around her and tell her not to be scared. But Bertha had become convinced that a human had to be responsible for the child's latest ghost concoction.

"You are going with me to your grandmother's home," the Sister said. "Umia has to be informed that she is to stop filling your head with nonsense."

Amalonda pressed both hands on her stomach to suppress the tremors she felt there. At the moment she couldn't have cared less about the nun's intent. Her mind was cemented on a more important issue—stopping the shudders and tremors of her empty stomach. "Can I please have a candy first? I'm hungry. There's nothing to eat at home except chicken fat."

Bertha sighed. Her heart went out to the hungry child. She

couldn't imagine not having at least one decent meal a day. This little girl and the other children in her situation were lucky if they had a substantial meal once a week. Being a compassionate nun was one thing, but acting as a teacher, counselor, meal-giver, and part-time parent to these children was incredibly demanding, taxing, and heart-wrenching. However, Bertha would not have it any other way.

"Of course you can have a candy, and when we get to your grandmother's, I will see what I can do to help her budget her pension money in order to buy groceries."

A few moments later, Amalonda, clutching a banana-flavored lollipop, walked behind Sister Bertha and exited the schoolhouse. Sucking furiously on the candy, Amalonda climbed into the back seat of the seen-better-days cab.

Bertha sat in the passenger seat and gave the driver directions to Umia's home. The cab was hardly in motion when Amalonda squealed in excitement. "See, Sister, I'm not lying. The Virgin Mary, Shiya, is sitting next to me." Amalonda's index finger wagged frantically at the shadowy formation manifesting itself on the back seat. "You got me into trouble, lady," Amalonda whispered. "Now you have to get me out of it."

The nun twisted her body around and felt an unearthly chill overcome her. She swallowed hard in disbelief as she took in the apparition's image: wispy blonde hair and spell-binding green eyes that seemed to pierce right through her body. Bertha quickly righted herself, crossed herself, fixed her eyes forward, and repeated softly, "Satan, be gone. Satan, be gone."

The cab driver took his eyes off the road to stare at the mumbling nun clutching her rosary beads. "Did you say something, Sister?"

"No," she replied. "Please concentrate on your driving. We don't want to have an accident, now do we?"

The silence was not golden. A telepathic voice as clear as the driver's spoke inside Bertha's head and forced her to raise her hands to her ears. But her attempt to block sound on its way to her eardrums could not stop the transcendental phenomenon. "Don't be afraid, dear Bertha," the whispery voice said. "It's me, Shiya, and I'm happy to see that you are wearing the sandals I gave you."

Whack!

The sound of Bertha's head hitting the car's side window brought the vehicle to a halt. With his mouth agape, the cab driver was momentarily shocked into silence.

But his other passenger had a different reaction.

Amalonda's bare soles rushed into Umia's front yard. The flapping sound was thunderous. So was her screech. "Help, Grandma! Someone help me. Sister Bertha is dead."

The cab driver finally found his voice. "Send an ambulance to 3249 Khoali Street," he instructed his dispatcher.

"What's happened?"

"I'm not sure, but I think I have a dead woman in my cab."

The reply was inaudible.

CHAPTER THIRTEEN

The Holy Cross Infirmary,
thirty minutes later

BERTHA'S EYELIDS SLOWLY OPENED. She wondered, "Where am I?" Her head felt as if it had been bashed with a baseball bat. Her vision focused on the ER equipment that surrounded her. Reality hit home. "Oh, Lord above," she gasped. "I'm in a hospital." She had no clue how she had arrived there. She hadn't heard the screaming ambulance siren. Suddenly, snippets of recent events flooded her mind; they were as clean as a white hospital blanket. Had she had an out-of-body experience? Had she really heard a voice from the past?

A realization dawned on her. No one else could have known about the sandals except the person who had given them to her! At the top of her voice she called out, "Nurse!"

As the metal curtain rings glided across the privacy rod, Bertha faced a petite African woman wearing old-fashioned red-and-white nursing attire. "How are you feeling?" the RN asked.

"Not bad, thank you. Just a slight headache is all," Bertha replied pleasantly. Then she gave the nurse her explanation of events. "Nurse, I don't need treatment. It was just a fainting spell that was probably brought on by not eating breakfast. Sometimes I skip my morning meal. I get carried away with my duties, and food becomes an afterthought. It won't happen again. Now, what have you done with my shoes? I would like to leave now. I'm a teacher and my schoolchildren need me."

"I will fetch the doctor who saw you on arrival."

"I don't need a doctor."

"It is hospital rule, Sister. I can't let you get up until the doctor has had a word with you."

After the nurse exited the room, the hospital curtain remained open. Although Bertha was left alone with her thoughts, she was not *entirely* on her own. She nearly jumped out of her skin when a willowy form wearing a long, white gown unexpectedly manifested itself at the end of the hospital gurney. "I didn't mean to scare you, Bertha. And I'm sorry if I caused the lump on your head."

"You are not real," Bertha reassured herself. "You are the work of the Devil." She made the sign of the cross on her forehead. "Satan, you can't fool me. My soul is not for the taking. Be gone with you."

Bertha imagined she heard laughter and a persuasive reply. "Oh, dear Bertha, you must hear me out. Your life and those of the dying—those sentenced to death by the nasty AIDS virus—depend on it. I have all-seeing eyes, just like Chief Naboto and Anele. They stand beside me."

"No, they don't" Bertha countered. "I don't see them."

"Believe me. They *are* here. And Anele says, 'Don't fight the gift that is only given to *special* people. You and Amalonda are special. Naboto is telling me that it is a shame you have forgotten where you come from?'"

Bertha let out a resigned sigh. She had long dismissed, but not entirely forgotten, her childhood tribal ways ... teachings saying that the dead do walk besides the living ... and that they can influence them. Hadn't her mother told her that their ancestors shed their mortal bodies for unseen ones? Hadn't Bertha caught her mother talking to what appeared to be nothing more than fresh air?

Bertha's mother, Nthara, had explained her strange behavior to her frowning daughter. "Farida, my precious child, your grandmother wants you to know that bad times will come your way in the approaching years, but you will overcome them. She says that you have a magical strength inside you and have the gift of seeing those who have left this mortal world."

Now, drawn to her tribal past, everything Bertha had been taught in Catholicism was abruptly forgotten. It was as if her mind had suddenly been repossessed by the child she once was. A grown up Farida, not a Catholic nun, was impelled to extend her hand. She felt the cool touch of a person she never thought she would see again.

"Shiya, I want you to know that you have never left my heart. I think of the goodness you did for so many poor souls in Tswanas, including myself. And yes, I still wear the sandals you gave me because they connect me to a wonderful person. I know you survived Sliman's bullet because I was at your hospital bedside in Durban. How could we both have been so terribly deceived by this man? Maybe you have the answer now. But I must ask you how you entered the afterlife? Not by another bullet, I hope."

"No, my life ended by the brain tumor I told you about when we first met. But that's not the worst of it. I will walk this earth until my physical remains and soul become reunited as one. You see, my daughter, Brianna, whom you met at Anele's funeral, removed my bones from a sacred burial place and placed them elsewhere."

"Why did she do that?"

"Oh, humanly she had good reason. But spiritually her actions will be her undoing. She's a sweet girl, but she will continue to ride on the bitter bus until she realizes that life is too short to carry resentment in one's heart. But that's enough of that. Listen carefully, Bertha, and follow my instructions ..."

Bertha didn't notice another presence had entered the room.

An on-call doctor walked into the room and frowned. His patient had her arms outstretched and was talking to herself. It crossed his mind to order a brain scan. He walked toward her and, peering over his bifocals, got the shock of his life. It couldn't be? No ... Yes. It was! Dr. William Ungobo was dumfounded. Bertha was the last person he had expected to see after a twelve-year stretch. Even though she had physically aged, she looked like a breath of fresh air. Yet the memory of another time was still freshly imprinted in his mind—the bruises shaped like fingers that had discolored her body.

Returning to reality, Bertha greeted the medical caregiver. "Good morning, Doctor. I just had a dizzy spell. Now, if it is okay with you, I would like to be discharged. I've important work to do."

She hadn't recognized him.

Doctor William, his knees weak, hid his shock well. In a calm and professional voice, he replied, "From your examination notes by the doctor who admitted you, I see no reason to keep you here. But you do have a nasty bump on your forehead, and I feel you cannot leave this hospital unaided. Whom can I call for you?"

"Yes, there is someone you can call."

William didn't want to drink from the past's poison well, but he couldn't help it. What happened back then haunted his mind. What could he have done better? Why did he walk away so easily and leave Bertha dangling at the gates of hell? William wanted to rush back and tell her he was sorry, but guilt kept him immobilized. He watched her leave the ward.

Zepsiweli, now age eighteen, was a janitor at the school. After being contacted by the doctor, he arrived at the hospital and appeared at Bertha's side. He helped her to the waiting van he had borrowed and proceeded to take her back to the school. He had a special place in his heart for the woman who had known him as a child.

On the drive, Bertha said, "Zepsiweli, I have something to tell you, and you must keep it a secret. Okay?"

While keeping one hand on the steering wheel, Zepsiweli respectfully removed his baseball cap and answered in a playful voice, "Sister, how can I be of service to you?"

"You and I have another adventure coming up, just like we did when you were little."

Zepsiweli's smile was as wide as the Nile. His natural intuition led him to guess where they were going. "I bet that we're going back to the Umfolozi game reserve?"

Bertha nodded, but she needed reassurance. "Zepsiweli, you have to promise not to say a word to anyone about this. Okay?"

"Sure. One hundred percent," he said grinning broadly.

Earlier, while Zepsiweli had been waiting for the doctor to finalize Bertha's discharge papers, he recalled the day he had met Sister Bertha. He had been one of the many preschoolers who had thronged around her when she arrived on a camel. It had been a sight to see. The new teacher had been clothed in a peculiar fashion. She had been clinging to the huge animal for dear life, sitting on a saddle that appeared to be made for a midget.

In the days that followed her arrival, Zepsiweli couldn't wait to get up in the morning and attend her school. She was fun. When not teaching the kids to read and write, she played hide-and-seek with them and watched them during their swim breaks at the river. But one not-so-pleasant memory from his childhood wasn't ready to leave him anytime soon.

It happened eleven years ago.

It was around midnight, and an August full moon neared its zenith. In the Tswanas settlement, an aging diabetic man groaned, his internal plumbing desperate for relief. Natu rose from his bed and stepped outside. Moonlight danced over the straw thatched roofs of circular homesteads and onto his spray of golden urine. Natu vigorously shook his penis of the last few drops and was about to return to his bed when something caught his attention. What were those strange shapes lying not far from his discharge spot?

The old man's brows furrowed. Bending down for closer look, he was even more stumped. He saw nine sprawling village dogs with white, iridescent-looking froth congealed around their rigid muzzles. Natu, who had discovered Chief Naboto's body many years ago, scratched his head. He touched the neck of the leader of the pack, a large male. The dog was warm to the touch, but obviously not breathing.

Natu's head began to spin as he asked the obvious question: "What's going on here?" He happened to glance at the hut next to his—Anele's home. He noticed that the blanket door- curtain was missing. He spotted it a few feet away. The perplexed Natu decided to check it out. He poked his head into Anele's hut. It was dark inside, but he was able to make out two motionless shapes huddled on the bed. They looked fast asleep, but he called out anyway. "Anele, Shiya, you need to come and see this."

He received no reply.

"A gentle shake should do the trick," he thought.

Nothing.

Then he felt something warm and gooey adhering to his bare feet. After touching it and putting his finger to his nose, he knew it was blood. In a flash, he was out of Anele's hut and back in his own home, where he grabbed an oil lamp and lit it.

The bright lamplight left no doubt. His hollering awoke the village.

Insikazi, Anele's daughter by Lord Hallworthy, was the first to arrive. She rushed to the bed and let out the loudest banshee howl ever heard. The grisly scene, now aided by bright lamplight, displayed blood-drenched hair and blood-streaked lines down unmoving faces. Insikazi lifted her dead mother's head. "What kind of evil monster would do this to my mother and to my sister, Shiya?"

It was old Natu who offered a theory. "Somebody had to be very angry to do this—to shoot them at such close range." Unanswered questions lingered in the back of his mind: "Who was the killer? Why were Anele and Shiya attacked? Whom had they angered?"

It didn't take long before Anele's hut was crammed with tribespeople. Their lamenting cries could have been heard for miles.

The witch doctor, Sliman, who looked as if he had been out for an evening stroll, elbowed his way into the hut. He grabbed Anele's wrist, pressed it with two fingers, and then let go. She was in final sleep. He lifted Shiya's limp arm. His eyes widened. A hand mirror held under Shiya's nose began to fog. "Shiya's alive. I need more light. Fetch more lamps." He turned to the hovering

Natu. "Go and get my medicine bag."

Natu's bowed legs sprinted youthfully to Sliman's hut. Could Sliman save her? Yes, there was no doubt in Natu's mind. Like his deceased father, Twazli, the most revered of all witch doctors, Sliman had incredible magical healing powers.

One person in the death hut was in a state of disbelief. In her innocence, Vimbela pushed her way to the bed. "Why do you not open your eyes, *Umama* Anele?" she said, shaking the woman she called "Mother." Insikazi, her heart already suffocating with grief, removed Vimbela's fierce grasp, which was crimson with sticky blood. Insikazi had to find a way to make the simple woman understand. "Our *umama* now sleeps with the dead, Vimbela. She is not coming back."

Pounding her chest, Vimbela fled from the hut. Her sorrowful shrills shattered the early hours. Outside, she fell to her knees and wept. Although a torrent of tears flowed into her mouth, she implored, "Ugwele, sacred Wind God of Africa, take the breath from my body so that I can fly free with *Umama* Anele. And if this is not your wish, then help my special baby, Shiya. Please put the strong breath of Life in her body. She can't die. *Please ... Please ... Please ...*" Vimbela's brain shut down and her pleas grew silent. She lay still on the ground. For the moment, only the sound of her soft inhalations could be heard. Minutes later, all hell broke loose.

Inside Anele's hut, just steps away from the grief-stricken Vimbela, Insikazi, now numbed with shock, spoke to Sliman. "Wise witch doctor, please tell me who has done this terrible thing. I'm sure it is not one of us. Why someone from the outside would want to kill my mother and try to kill Shiya is a mystery? And why were our animals poisoned?"

"Is it not obvious, Insikazi," Sliman responded. "How else could the killer enter the village and get to the women?"

.

"But it doesn't make sense. I am a light sleeper," Insikazi said. "I heard no dogs bark in the night."

"Ah! You wouldn't have," Sliman said with authority. "The killer knew the animals well. They didn't fear him, but he caused their mouths to close, just in case."

Insikazi was so upset at that time that his words flew by her, temporarily unabsorbed. Only later did they have meaning. From the horse's mouth would come the most startling of revelations.

Zepsiweli, who was fidgeting on the hospital bench waiting for Sister Bertha to be discharged, had been involved in what took place after the discovery of the shooting victims. His memory kicked back in.

From seemingly nowhere, a boy, small enough to wriggle through the thronging crowd, pushed his way to the center of the activity. His hands were on his hips as he haughtily announced, "I know who killed Anele and the *umlungu* woman named Shiya." Both Sliman's and Insikazi's eyes pounced on the little boy. "Explain at once, Zepsiweli," Insikazi demanded, as she grabbed the boy roughly by the shoulders. Her nails dug deep.

"Ouch. That hurts," Zepsiweli cried, as he writhed in her fierce grasp. "I saw with my own eyes old man Kelingo and the *umlungu* man, the one who comes in the big bird that falls from the sky."

"Your head is full of worms, boy. Old Kelingo! Never! He never would have harmed my mother or Shiya. He loved them, and ..."

She didn't get a chance to probe further into the most important part of the boy's declaration—the involvement of the bush pilot, Captain Johannes de Klerk. She focused on Natu, who was handing over Sliman's baboon-hide bag.

Although no one spoke, all eyes were glued on the witch doctor.

With the sharp point of a hunting knife, Sliman tried to

determine how far the bullet was lodged in Shiya's wound. Feeling no metal on metal, he withdrew the knife. He filled the hole with a mixture of muddy-looking, bad-smelling ointment. The elderly Natu held up Shiya's head, and the medicine man bandaged it with long lengths of deer hide. They lifted Shiya off the blood-spattered bed and rested her body on the dirt floor. The cold, damp earth would slow down her heart rate, the witch doctor explained. Then Sliman cut the little bag Shiya wore around her neck and released the stones onto the floor. He stared at the multicolored stones as they gradually began changing to one shade—bright turquoise. "It's a great sign," he announced. "Her spirit is not ready to fly away.

Behind him, bystanders debated on who had done this terrible deed. One elderly woman had her say: "In my heart, I feel that the boy speaks the truth. Old Kelingo *is* the traitor, even if he didn't pull the trigger. He only pretended to love his people and the woman who saved him from the white man's work."

"He belongs to the Dark Spirit now," said another.

Bertha's presence in the hut brought the chatter to a halt. She was not half-naked, as were the rest, but instead was wearing a long, cotton nightshirt that flowed over her bare feet. "What's going on in here?" Bertha questioned. "And does anyone know why Vimbela is screaming her head off loudly enough to wake the dead."

Intense high-pitched wailing now came from Insikazi. Her sobbing was as passionate as Vimbela's and ran through the schoolteacher's veins like hyperthermia. Was she sleepwalking? Bertha noticed Natu's gesture. His finger pointed to the floor. "God have mercy!" Bertha cried, rushing to the prone figure. "Someone please tell me what's going on," she demanded as she bent down to take a closer look at Shiya. "Why is she covered in blood?"

Sliman explained, "They both have been shot."

Bertha didn't wait for a further explanation. She dashed to the bed where the dead Anele lay. While her tears fell, the nun placed her index finger on Anele's clammy forehead and made the sign of the cross. Even though she knew Anele was a nonbeliever, Bertha silently gave Anele her last rites. Then the nun lifted the dead woman's hand, placed it to her lips and kissed it, saying, "Farewell, dear friend. I will get to the bottom of this. I promise. Justice will be done."

Bertha turned, seeking out a familiar face. "Ah, there you are. Zepsiweli," she said as she took the boy's hand. "I want you to go and get dressed. Then get the mules from behind the cowshed and take them to the back gate. I'll be along in a minute."

"Where are we going, Teacher?"

"We are going to get help for the poor woman who is very sick. Now run along and do as you are told?"

Like a sirocco wind, the boy blew from the hut.

Sliman approached Bertha. His long fingers latched firmly onto her wrist. The icy contact sent shivers down her spine. "We don't need *outside* intervention," he emphasized snippily. He let go of his grip, focused on the ground, and continued. "I'm a gifted medicine man. I will heal Shiya's wounds ... make her whole again ... and I don't need a Catholic nun's permission to do so. You stick to what you know best—praying to statues and playing with beads—and I will do my *heathen* job," he ended insultingly, letting her know that he did not acknowledge her God of the Bible.

Bertha wasn't the confrontational type, but her rigid body language said it all. She had never liked this pompous man, not from the moment she had laid eyes on him. And her dislike was not because of his offensive ways. No. There was something about this arrogant man she could not put her finger on. She remembered what her mother had once said about her father, Sani: "Farida, never trust a man whose eyes are too close together. When he looks at his feet when talking to you, he is lying to you. A good man will never take his eyes off you when he has something good or bad to say."

Bertha, now hot under the collar, spoke her mind: "Sliman, a crime has been committed here. I must notify the authorities. Zepsiweli and I will travel to the game reserve, to the white warden's home, and get help for Shiya. After all, she is *white!*"

"So you think that's wise," Sliman sneered. "We have no real witness. As sure as the sun rises in the east, one of *us* will be blamed for this because, yes, Shiya is *umlungu* ..."

"No one is going to accuse us," Bertha argued. "None of us shot the women. We have no guns here."

"You are wrong, schoolteacher," Sliman said with a smirk. He toyed with her sarcastically as he added, "How do you know I don't sleep with a gun under my pillow?"

Goosebumps erupted on the skin of Bertha's exposed arm.

"And would your God remove the bullet still lodged in her brain? I doubt it."

Bertha had heard enough. She turned on her heels. In her own hut, not far from the tragedy, she bent down and removed a suitcase from under her bed. She selected some items to wear. It had been a long while since she had donned her habit and headdress, but if ever there was a need to do so, it was now. "Yes," she uttered. Her official garb was needed to make her look credible. Who in their right mind would doubt a nun's word?

Bertha ran like a windstorm to the back gate, where Zepsiweli and the mules were waiting. Even though she was glad her transport wasn't a camel, she knew a mule wasn't as accommodating.

Having difficulties mounting in a long dress, she grabbed

the mule's ear by mistake, and *wallop*. She landed unladylike on her backside. Zepsiweli laughed so hard his insides hurt. After receiving a harsh glare, he helped Bertha remount the feisty horse mule. Holding her reins and his, the hardy boy led the mules from the kraal and onto a moonlit trail, a pathway he could navigate blindfolded. From the age of four, his father had taken him on poaching raids that utilized this track.

With Bertha and Zepsiweli long gone, Insikazi knelt beside her mother's bed and softly said, "I know in my heart that you do not fly free. Please give me a sign that you remain earthbound?"

As though granting her request, an eagle's feather drifted into the hut and spiraled onto the foot of the bed. Anele's heartbroken daughter picked it up, held it over her heart, and murmured, "*Umama*, you sent me a sign. Your killer has not taken your spirit, only the vessel that carried you on this earth." She leaned forward and placed the feather in her mother's blood- spattered hair. "I promise you this, *Umama*: I will hunt Kelingo, the snake he is, if it takes me the rest of my life. I will kill him with my bare hands. I swear it to you, my beloved mother."

She could not have been more wrong about the man she assumed was her mother's killer! But she was not the only one who was mistaken. Another person would also be blindsided by the identity of the killer.

Detective Marquand, the crime-scene investigator, had the wool pulled over his investigative eyes. His open-and-shut case was totally wrong!

Much later, newspapers, radio broadcasts, and TV shows would cry foul.

CHAPTER FOURTEEN

Bertha's secretive mission, 2009

AFTER BERTHA'S BRIEF HOSPITAL VISIT, she and Zepsiweli entered the school grounds. Sister Claudia rushed to greet her. "Sister, how are you? I was so worried when I got the news from Amalonda. I wasn't expecting you back so soon."

"Just a fainting spell, Sister, but I'm perfectly fine now."

"I'm glad to hear that. Is there anything I can do for you? Make you a cup of tea?"

"Thank you, but no. I have something I need to do, and I need you to take charge of the school. I'll be back sometime tomorrow, if all goes well. And if you are asked by anyone where I am, tell them I've gone out of town on urgent business."

Sister Claudia frowned. Something wasn't right, but she did not press the matter further. "Of course, Sister," she said. "I'd better hurry back to the classroom now before the little angels get up to mischief."

With Claudia out of earshot, Bertha turned to Zepsiweli. "Wait outside. I have a telephone call to make. I will figure out the bus times and then join you."

Zepsiweli nodded and left. Within seconds he was back. "Sister, there's a man outside. He says he must see you. It's urgent."

Bertha went to the side door and greeted the stranger. "Good afternoon. How can I help you?"

"Good afternoon, Sister. My name is Mandegizi Umdaba. We spoke on the phone." He dug into his pocket and held out the reason he was there. "These adornments belonged to Vimbela of the Ancients. I'd like you to have them. Do with them what you will."

Bertha felt warm tears sting the back of her eyes as she clutched the only possessions left of the woman she had failed to help. Bertha showed her gratitude to Mandegizi sincerely. "I can't thank you enough, Mr. Umdaba. You have come all this way to return precious items belonging to our dearly loved Vimbela."

"I tried my best, Sister, but she was stubborn. Who would have thought that a snake could have ended her fight to save all that was sacred to her. I would have driven her here myself if she had let me."

Bertha noticed his beat-up truck parked near the rear entrance. Her heart began to beat like a drum. For a second, the vehicle resurrected a painful memory. But she quickly turned her head toward Mandegizi and brought her thoughts to the present day: "Will he? Does he have the time? Can he be trusted?" Bertha felt impelled to ask him a question: "Mr. Umdaba, I was wondering if you could do me a favor. You see, I need to return to Tswanas, or should I say where the Tswanas village once was. Could I hire you to drive me there?"

Her request was immediately met with a favorable response.

"It would be my pleasure, Sister." Mandegizi rubbed his forehead. It was none of his business, but he found himself asking, "Why do you want to go there? There's nothing left of the village or the burial grounds. And it would be dangerous now. The beasts are already roaming free."

"Mr. Umdaba ..."

"Excuse me, Sister. Call me Mandegizi."

"Very well. 'Mandegizi' it is." Bertha added sweetly, "I will explain once we get there, but my mission there is to be kept a secret. You must tell no one. Do I have your word?"

"Of course, Sister," he replied. "When would you like to go?"

Her answer came urgently and swiftly. "*Now*."

Looking surprised, Mandegizi repeated, "Now?" He noticed the look of anxiety creasing Bertha's face, and he yielded. "It's okay by me, but I'm not a rich man, Sister, so I must ask if you have the money for petrol. My old truck is always thirsty, and it will take many fuel-ups to go that distance."

Bertha turned to Zepsiweli, who had not left her side. "Go and get my shoulder bag from the locker in the back room, and bring it to me." Then, facing Mandegizi, she steered the conversation away from their impending trip and the painful questions she had about Vimbela's last moments. "Do you live here in Soweto? Is your family here? Are you married? How many children do you have?"

Mandegizi gave short answers, but Bertha was surprised when he mentioned a name she knew all too well: Konoye. Of course, she wanted to tell this kindhearted man that his brother was nothing more than a crook, but she held her tongue. She was sure that Mandegizi would find out soon enough.

With a tinge of guilt and without divulging too much, Sister Bertha handed a wad of notes (the school's candy fund) to

Mandegizi saying, "This is all I have, and I hope it is enough for our journey."

"Don't worry, Sister. If it isn't enough, I'll add my own money to it."

"Oh, that's so good of you. And I will certainly repay you as soon as I can."

Mandegizi smiled. "I'll go and fuel up and be back shortly, Sister."

Bertha watched the old truck sputter into action and head down the road. Then she and Zepsiweli went inside to prepare for the journey. As instructed by the nun, he found two shovels and several flashlights. Bertha packed a basket with bottled water, a loaf of crusty bread, a block of cheese, and a few oranges.

Twenty minutes later, the three adventurers were huddled together on the front seat of Mandegizi's truck and heading down back roads that would lead them out of Soweto.

None of them could have guessed that this get-rich adventure would seal their fates for their remaining days on Earth.

CHAPTER FIFTEEN

The Umfolozi Game Reserve, eight and a half hours later

IT WAS ALMOST MIDNIGHT when the weary travelers arrived at the designated location. Thankfully, they were not spotted entering the reserve. Except for Mandegizi's, they had seen no other headlights for miles.

Acting on Bertha's instructions to "ask no questions and tell no lies," Mandegizi began digging, but it was no easy task. The metal blade of the shovel protested against the cement-like, arid earth that encircled the massive and ancient baobab—Chief Naboto's revered tree. The Chief's incisions marking the birth and death of his children were barely visible under the beam of the flashlight.

Zepsiweli also obeyed Bertha's instructions. High in the tree, he acted as the lookout for two-legged and four-legged predators. Since the game reserve had extended its boundaries and introduced more wild animals, poaching was ubiquitous, worse even than in the days of the Tswanas tribe, which had had to kill many animals to survive. This new breed of poachers was despised by all. But as long as there was a demand for ivory and rhinoceros horn, there would be unconscionable traders.

With her flashlight in hand, Bertha watched the digging unfold. Deep down she didn't want to learn that her impulsive desire to find Shiya's buried treasure was a figment of her imagination; that everything she had perceived had, in reality, been a dream; that she was giving the devil a foothold by not telling the truth; and that she had allowed one of the deadly sins—greed—to overtake her good soul.

Bertha's mind quickly justified her actions. "Just think how much good could be done with an abundance of money, the many people who could be saved by antiviral medication. Hadn't Shiya commented that her jewels were worth a fortune?" But missing from her euphoria was stark reality. Bertha had not considered ahead of time that selling jewels without the owner's permission was a criminal offense and that sooner, rather than later, Mandegizi would put two and two together. His elated cry, "I think I've found something," cut short her conflicting thoughts.

With excitement tingling through her veins, Bertha hurried to his side. She heard the clunk of metal and saw the airtight, silver-plated tea caddy. She pried the rusty lid open with a screwdriver taken from Mandegizi's truck.

"Oh, my God!" she exclaimed, staring at the contents in the removable pewter insert. "It wasn't a dream. I didn't imagine it."

Exquisite pieces of 18-karat gold, diamond, ruby, emerald, and pearl jewelry glittered in the beam of a flashlight.

It was Mandegizi who burst the jubilation bubble. "Who does this belong to? Whoever it is, they must be notified of our find."

"I can't do that, Mandegizi," Bertha softly replied. "I knew the owner very well, and she is dead. She came to me in a vision and told me where to find her jewelry. She asked me to sell the pieces to save my people."

Mandegizi scratched his sweaty forehead. "Well I hope she put that in writing before she died?"

"No, she didn't."

"Not that I want any part of this, but the only place you can fence this stuff is to sell it to black market dealers. And I can assure you, they will take you to the cleaners if you don't know the value."

Bertha took hold of Mandegizi's hand and responded, "We should pray, ask God to guide us."

"Sister, I'm a churchgoing man. Yet while I respect your desire to ask God for guidance, our Lord cannot be party to something that is against His law and the law of man. The dead woman you speak of must have family. It is from the family that permission must be sought."

Bertha nodded. "Yes, you are right. I know Shiya has a daughter. I met her at Chief Anele's funeral. But I have no idea where she is." It was Bertha's turn to scratch her head. "Ah. There might be a way to find her. I still have the address of a reporter who came to document the assassination of Anele and the attempted murder of Shiya. His name is Winston Mandekana. Yes. That's what I have to do ... try to locate the whereabouts of Shiya's daughter, Brianna."

Mandegizi nodded his approval. Even Zepsiweli, who had stayed out of the discussion, nodded. He loved Sister Bertha and didn't want anything bad to happen to her if she disregarded Mandegizi's warnings.

After tucking the tea caddy and its treasures into her picnic basket, Bertha, her driver, and her lookout got into the truck and headed back the way they had come.

Bertha had one request before returning to Soweto. "Mandegizi, can we stop at the gravesite? I would like to return Vimbela's ankle adornments to her. According to her beliefs, her spirit won't rest unless I return the bracelets that were meant to be carried with her into the afterlife."

"Oh, I don't think that's wise, Sister. That area of fencing is *definitely* patrolled. If we are stopped, how are we going to explain our presence in a restricted area? And someone may recognize me. I worked on that project."

Bertha pondered his statement for a moment. "It's the blackest night I have seen in a long while. No one will see us. Please, Mandegizi, take me. I have to do this."

Bertha placed Vimbela's bracelets deep into the earth and was saying a prayer for the departed when, suddenly, all hell broke loose. Illuminated by the blinding headlights of several vehicles, Bertha and Mandegizi froze on the spot. Zepsiweli, whimpering, threw himself under the old truck.

Uniformed men with guns drawn stepped from the vehicles. One of them issued a command that resonated loudly. "Put your hands in the air where I can see them."

Bertha, her knees shaking, called out. "My name is Sister Bertha. I'm a Catholic nun from Soweto." She glibly added, "I'm with my driver. He lost his way bringing me back from the market in Pongola."

With two patrol vehicles in front of their truck and two behind, the shaking, silent occupants were escorted out of the game reserve.

Not a word crossed any of their lips until they arrived back home in Soweto a little before 12:30 P.M. Only then did Bertha speak. "Mandegizi, I can't thank you enough for taking me on this journey, and I pray that not a word will be said about it."

"You have my word, Sister," his tired voice returned.

Bertha turned to the shaken Zepsiweli and handed him what was left of the petrol money. "Take this and buy yourself some lunch. Don't report for work until tomorrow."

Bertha watched Mandegizi's truck drive down the dusty road. Then she entered the school grounds. She had forgotten that it was lunchtime, and a swarm of children surrounded her. One in particular grabbed her hand. Amalonda asked, "Where have you been, Sister Bertha? I've been looking for you. I wanted to tell you that my grandmother is in the hospital. My cousin says she is dying. They won't let me in to see her. Please take me to her."

Bertha clasped a hand over her mouth. Had she let this Tswanas woman down, as she had Vimbela? Hadn't she promised to call on Umia from time to time? She hadn't made it to Umia's front door before she, herself, had ended up in the hospital.

Could the monetary proceeds made from the jewelry she possessed buy the costly antiviral medication needed to save Umia's life? Maybe ... but probably not.

Bertha's intention to wash, change out of dirty clothing, and head for the hospital with Amalonda was thwarted by a telephone call. "I would like to speak to Sister Bertha, please," a male voice said.

"This is Sister Bertha. How can I help you?"

William's heart missed a beat. Her voice was enthrallingly soft. He gave himself a mental slap. Now was not the time to have heart jitters. "This is Doctor William from the Holy Cross Infirmary. I'm sorry to inform you that Umia of Tswanas died in the night. Before her passing, she begged me to get in contact with you and relay her fears for the well-being of her granddaughter, Amalonda. Umia worried that if Amalonda is left in the hands of her lazy, good-for-nothing, alcoholic relatives, she will be neglected. Because Umia's pension dies with her, she feared that Amalonda will die without medication. She did mention that a special friend to both of you, a person by the name of Shiya, says that you do not need permission to sell her things and help others' lives. I hope this makes sense?"

"Yes, it does. Thank you for calling."

"Oh, before you hang up, there is the matter of the release of her body for burial. It seems she had no money, and as she is a friend of yours, I thought it prudent to offer to pay these expenses out of my own pocket."

"Why on earth would you do that?" Bertha swallowed hard. Oh, I don't mean to sound rude, but you hardly knew Umia."

"But I know *you*."

Bertha's face scrunched in puzzlement before she gave a confused response. "How can you know me? We never met until yesterday."

"No, Sister. That is where you are wrong. We have met in another place and another time."

"I don't want to contradict you, but I'm positive I have never met you before now."

There was a long silence before William spilled the beans. "Sister, I'm the doctor who treated you after the rape ..."

Bertha, her face ashen, dropped the phone.

"Are you there," William's voice asked.

Bertha picked up the dangling receiver and hung up on the caller. Her thoughts were tumultuous. She reeled with the explosive discovery. It was *him* whom she had seen yesterday hanging around the school after her brief hospital stay. It must have been *him* who had anonymously sent expensive chocolates and a floral bouquet to the school. No one else she knew could have afforded these luxuries. The whys and wherefores remained unanswered. After all she was a nun. Nuns didn't have would-be suitors. Her "arranged" marriage of religious belief had taken place years ago.

Bertha dashed from the hallway into her bedroom. She locked

the door and sat on the cot. With the past clawing its way back into her head, she sobbed into her hands—tears galore. Everything she thought was long gone and buried rose within her like the mythical phoenix. Now she was living the nightmarish ordeal all over again. As she cradled her head, a stampede of what-to-do-next thoughts raced through her mind. She uttered not one prayer, and she refused to open her door to anyone, not even a concerned Claudia, who bent down and spoke through the keyhole.

"Sister, please open the door."

"No."

"Would you like me to call a priest?"

"Definitely not!"

"Sister, I can't bear to hear you cry. Something must be dreadfully wrong. I want to be of help."

Bertha sighed. "That's kind of you, Sister. But I need time to think."

Claudia prayed. Bertha did not.

In the wee hours of the morning, her faith had been tested over and over, and something inside Bertha broke. She realized that she had made the biggest mistake of her life. But what choice had she? She had been handed over to the nuns as if she were nothing more than a lost-and-found object. Without a doubt, she had been brainwashed into thinking that Christianity held all the keys to a good life. Were Muslim teachings any better?

She began to pack.

"I'm not done yet. I'm not dead," she confirmed to herself.

Shortly before seven o'clock the next morning, Sister Claudia discovered the neatly folded habits and religious apparel that had belonged to Bertha. Rosary beads and a small silver crucifix lay nearby. On the top of the clothing Claudia found a note: *My faith in God is dead. My faith in humanity is dead. My faith now lies in healing my broken self. Somewhere down the road I forgot who Bertha really is. Her name is Farida. I'm going home.*

"I have a dream today." Bertha ended with a Martin Luther King, Jr., quote.

CHAPTER SIXTEEN

Bertha's and Amalonda's getaway, December 20, 2009, five days after Umia's death

"You can never plan the future by the past ..."
—Edmund Burke

THERE WERE HARDLY ANY FOLK or traffic about on this very early Sunday morning in Nancefield. The defecting nun was thankful for that. But soon there would be stirring—people getting ready to attend Sunday Mass or other religious attendances. However, Bertha was somewhat confident that no one would recognize her in her new getup. She had metamorphosed: shed her "penguin" attire for the makings of a colorful butterfly.

Wearing a bright, yellow-and-orange-spattered, front-buttoned kaftan made of cashmere that she had removed from a bag of clothing donated to the school, plus an orange headscarf that hid her hair stubble, Bertha made her way toward Umia's home.

She rapped on Umia's front door and continued knocking until the door finally opened.

Umia's young relative, rubbing sleep from his eyes, glared at Bertha. "Lady, do you know what time it is? It's five o'clock, dammit. What the hell do you want?"

"I'm sorry to wake you at this hour," she apologized diplomatically. "But I need to see Amalonda."

"She's asleep."

"Can you wake her? It's important."

"What the hell could be so damn important that you need to speak to a child at this hour? Can't it wait?"

It was obvious from his slurred speech that he was hungover. Bertha wasn't about to be messed with; however, she decided to tread carefully. "I knew her grandmother very well, and I want to support Amalonda in her hour of grief."

His flat facial expression told Bertha that he was in no mood to play host. He wanted her gone so he could go back to sleep. After what seemed an eternity, he caved in, "Okay. Wait here. I'll get her."

Amalonda, with her eyes puffy from crying and her crumpled lime-green miniskirt and top suggesting she had slept in her clothing, squinted at the woman stood in the doorway. Then the penny dropped, and sentence after sentence pounced on Bertha at cyclone speed. "Wow, Sister! I didn't recognize you. Why are you wearing a pretty dress? What are you doing here? Have you come to say goodbye to grandma? She's not here. She's at the hospital. They won't let me see her dead body."

Her distant cousin had long turned away leaving Bertha and Amalonda alone. Bertha snatched the opportunity. She bent down and whispered in Amalonda's ear. "Listen to me and ask no questions. Okay? Go quietly get a change of clothing and your medicine. You are coming with me."

Amalonda's brows furrowed. "Where are we going?"

"You don't need to know that at this moment, child. Hurry now. It's for your own good. Get your stuff, Amalonda, and meet me down the alleyway as soon as you can."

While Amalonda scooted off like a thief in the night, Bertha made her way around the back of the shack and waited a few yards in the designated spot. Time was of the essence. Bertha wanted to be long gone before someone else recognized her.

The thudding of Amalonda's rubber-made sandals was music to Bertha's ears. The child hadn't been stopped by the grumpy relative who had opened the door.

"Sister, are we going on an adventure?" she asked excitedly, handing Bertha a pair of unwashed pink shorts and a white top.

"In a way, child, but you have to trust me. Okay? Where's your medicine?"

"There's none left. My grandmother ..." Her eyes filled with tears. "... had no money to buy some for me, and now she has gone to heaven. I'm supposed to take the pills twice a day, or I will die like my grandma."

Bertha hugged the bewildered-looking child clinging to her side. "Don't worry. You are not going to die if I can help it. I'll buy the pills for you as soon as I find an open pharmacy. You are going to be fine. I'm going to take good care of you. And you are not going to end up in some awful orphanage like I did years ago." Bertha turned her head away from Amalonda's wide, probing eyes. Bertha knew in her heart that sooner or later the deadly virus would claim this tiny victim, but not yet.

"I trust you, Sister," Amalonda said, "and the lady in the wedding dress. She came to me in my dreams and told me I was going to be saved."

"What?" It took Bertha a couple of seconds to fathom the girl's words. "You mean Shiya."

"Yes, Shee-I-ya. You believe me now, don't you, Sister?"

"Yes, I do, but Amalonda, I need you to keep a secret."

"I love secrets," she responded eagerly.

"First, you must call me Mama Farida, not Sister Bertha. I'm not a nun anymore. And if anyone asks, I'm your mother."

Amalonda pulled a comical face and then looked at Bertha with an expression that said, "I'm just a kid. I don't think like an adult, but I'm going to nod anyway." Nonetheless, this was a nice secret to keep. She had longed for a mother ever since she had been told hers had died in childbirth.

Holding Bertha's hand tightly, Amalonda repeatedly mouthed, "Mama Farida. Mama Farida." It was a happy moment for a child who, until now, had lost everything.

Bertha, wearing Shiya's sandals, took hold of her "daughter's" hand and began walking down the back alleys toward the main road leading out of the township. But their footsteps weren't the only ones leaving the area. If either of them had turned around, they would have seen an eagle feather floating down from the sky. It was as silent as the footsteps moving beyond the mortal plane.

On the last block of the town, Bertha spotted a sign: "Pawn Broker." The heavily barred shop was lit from within. An "Open" sign was displayed on the steel security entrance door. Bertha couldn't have been more pleased, even though she had never noticed a business of this kind open at 5:30 A.M., especially on a Sunday. She refrained from using the adage "God walks in mysterious ways ..." because she had purposely wandered away from God and was numb to the core with doubt. Yes, she had a huge hill to climb to eradicate many years of a put-upon religion. But for now, she had to revitalize her spunk!

Should she risk it? Would too many questions be asked? "How did you come by this expensive item?" Would the owner call the police? Would she be arrested for possessing suspected "stolen" property? Bertha had to think fast if she was going to make it work.

"Amalonda, wait here by the door," she ordered. "I have to see a man in this store." She pointed, and ended with, "Don't move a muscle. I won't be long."

A noisy overhead bell announced her presence. The proprietor, a short, tubby man, adjusted his eye-glasses and weighed up Bertha as she made her way to the counter. All walks of life had crossed his path, but there was something about this attractive woman, aside from her hippie-fashioned long garment with elbow-length sleeves, that spiked his curiosity. "What can I do for you?"

Bertha dug into her "donated," gold-colored, basket-weave shoulder bag. From a zippered compartment she withdrew the tea caddy. Discreetly, she removed a pearl necklace and placed it on the glass countertop. "How much can you give me for this?"

The pawnbroker looked at her like a bad rash before examining the antique, thirty-seven-inch pearl necklace with an 18-carat-gold diamond clasp. He had never seen anything so fine, but he wasn't going to let on. "Well, that all depends on if this necklace is genuine, and ..." Peering over his glassed he added, "... and not stolen property."

"Oh, I can guarantee it's not stolen," Bertha asserted. "A dear friend gave it to me before she died."

"Do you have that in writing?" he asked sarcastically.

"No, I don't. So are we going to do business or not?" Bertha returned with an air of arrogance.

The pawnbroker stared at Bertha and scratched his head. The more he looked at her the more he felt he knew her. "Nah," his head told him. Then he set about reexamining the string of antique pearls for flaws, scratches, or other damage. There were none. He could make a bundle of money on this necklace, but he had to deal with a woman who was obviously intelligent. He threw out a low offer: "Three hundred and eighty rand is the best I can do."

Bertha gritted her teeth and glared at the greed-monger. She did not recognize him, even though she had butted heads with Konoye, Mandegizi's rent-robbing brother. "You have to do better than that!" Bertha barked. "I may look an idiot, but I can assure you I am not. Your ridiculous offer (fifty dollars) is an insult to my intelligence."

Konoye heaved a long sigh. "Okay. I'll give you a break, lady. I will double my offer, but that's as far as I'll go. Take it or leave it. It's up to you."

From behind them, a man wearing a two-tone blue uniform and a dress cap in darker blue approached the counter. Bertha quickly nodded her acceptance of the puny monetary offer. The policeman would have probable cause to arrest her if the pawnbroker aired his suspicions.

Bertha hurriedly placed the wad of notes into her brassiere and marched out the door. She felt angry and a tad guilty, but she needed the money. And, she wasn't sure if the other man in the room was a police officer or a security guard.

From a nearby street vendor, Bertha bought a smoked sausage, a can of Coke, and a packet of lollipops for Amalonda. Her happy, delighted smile was worth every penny. A bottle of iced green tea was Bertha's breakfast. Tummy rumbles were the furthest things from her mind. All she was worried about now was whether she had enough to buy Amalonda's antiviral combination pills, the ones that were administered at school to those whose parents couldn't afford the lifesaving drugs? Bertha was aware of the effects on Amalonda if her medication wasn't administered. She had lost count of the number of times the girl had to be rushed to hospital for abdominal pain, vomiting, diarrhea, and weakness. And it boiled down to Umia's pension money being spent on the rent.

Now, Bertha had to do what she had to do.

Leaving Amalonda in the care of the friendly female street vendor, Bertha rushed back to the grubby little pawnbroker. Konoye was more than delighted when she handed over a gold and diamond-encrusted wedding band. This time, no questions or comments were made. A good deal was struck, and Bertha walked out of the shop with a pleased smile on her face, not an angry grimace.

"Come back any time, Sister," she heard him say. His recognition was lost on Bertha. She had only one thing on her mind.

The hot rising sun was bearing down on the pair as they entered a pharmacy. With Amalonda happily window shopping, Bertha headed for the dispensing counter.

"Good morning. How can I help you?"

Bertha handed the pharmacist a slip of paper detailing the drug therapy needs of both herself and Amalonda. In her haste, Bertha had left behind the pain medicine that kept her back condition in check.

The pharmacist scanned the requirements and then promptly handed the note back to Bertha. He tried to be soft, kind, and understanding. "I'm sorry, but I can't dispense these meds without a prescription from your doctor."

"My daughter is sick," Bertha protested. "She needs this medicine. I'm worried she is going to die without treatment. It's Sunday. My doctor's office is closed, and this can't wait until tomorrow."

"Sorry, but that's the rule," he said professionally. "No doctor's prescription. No pills."

Bertha was at a low point—frustrated by helplessness. For a split second she contemplated saying a prayer. Old habits do die hard. In the end, though, Bertha scoffed at the idea. She had suffered three major traumas in her life. First, the circumcision; second, the village massacre that resulted in the loss of everyone she ever knew as well as her physical home and surroundings; third, an excruciatingly painful rape. Throughout all of this, *He* had never come to her aid. So why would He help her now?

But it wasn't game over! *There is a silver lining to every dark cloud.*

A husky voice from behind her said, "Maybe I can be of help." Bertha turned and her face drained. Her body immediately shut down.

Her rapist's father grabbed her before she hit the concrete floor.

CHAPTER SEVENTEEN

The tourist town of Siavonga, Republic of Zambia, four days later

ON A HILLSIDE AT THE NORTH END of Lake Kariba, William's four-bedroom stucco, fieldstone, and rough-hewn timber retirement home was bathed in a stunning sunset.

Smoking his pipe, the elderly William couldn't have been more relaxed as he sat in a rocking chair on his wraparound porch. He never dreamed he would acquire "replacements" for all he had lost—the tragic deaths of his wife and baby daughter, which still haunted him, even now, almost twelve years later.

After that dreadful night in January 1998 when he had been summoned by his son, Samuel, to attend to Bertha's injuries, William had returned to his apartment morally and physically devastated. All he could see was Bertha's bruised face and her eyes, which were pleading for him to save her. He was so haunted by what had happened that he made up his mind then and there. And so, two weeks later, he closed his prosperous clinic without explanation to his staff. Deep down, he wanted to make a fresh start, away from the egregious behavior of his son from a former marriage.

But the day before his relocation to Soweto to take up his new posting at Holy Cross Infirmary, tragedy struck him down like a shotgun bullet.

He was packing his clothes when the doorbell rang.

His heart skipped a beat when he saw two uniformed policemen.

"Are you Doctor Ungobo?"

Being scientifically minded, an adrenalin surge of questions besieged him. Had Bertha filed a report? Had she named him as an accessory? Had Samuel been arrested? Were the cops here to arrest him, too? "Yes, I'm Doctor Ungobo," William responded with composure. "What can I do for you?"

"Doctor, I'm sorry to inform you that your wife and baby daughter are dead, along with the reckless drunk driver who hit them in a head-on collision on Mombasa Street."

William's capable mind went into a tailspin of disbelief. His wife's voice was still clear in his head: "I won't be long, darling. I'm taking Sadie and heading for the store. I want to buy a good supply of diapers before we leave."

"I can drive you," he had offered.

His wife had smiled. "It's okay, darling. I need to get other things, such as hair shampoo. I'll be back in an hour."

After the accident, the grieving doctor had questioned God: Why had He taken the lives of these innocent victims when Samuel was presumably still breathing his evil upon Earth? Yes, Samuel had entered the clergy at much too young an age—pressured into it by his mother. William had been dead set against it, but he, too, came under pressure from his former wife. What had caused Samuel's perverted sexual derangement? William could only guess. As far as William was aware, Samuel had never experimented with sex before entering the minor seminary at age twelve.

After the funeral, a lost William headed for the Holy Cross Infirmary in Soweto. There, he was welcomed with open arms. Not many qualified specialists came through their doors willing to take a pay cut. And very few medical students were available. A costly education was beyond the reach of most people who had the desire to enter a medical practice in KwaZulu Natal. William's parents had worked their fingers to the bone to send him to the School of Medicine at the University of Nairobi. His interest in gynecology, birthing—in women and their medical sufferings— led him to specialize in obstetrics. Eventually, he opened his own clinic on the outskirts of Nairobi.

Now retired, William didn't have the pressure of trying to establish himself in the world, professionally or economically. But he did feel empty. What he wanted to do now was devote all of his time to Bertha (Farida), find areas of communication with an equal, and develop a loving relationship. He also wanted both of them to focus on the little girl they would raise together. They were his family now. And he couldn't have cared less about the well-being of Samuel. The last he had heard, Samuel got what he deserved—a lengthy prison sentence. William hoped he would receive help for his sexual addiction, but he somehow doubted it. In his opinion, Samuel was just born wicked.

Now, here he was 1,300 kilometers upstream from the Indian Ocean along the border of Zimbabwe. With one of the Seven Wonders of the World, Victoria Falls, in the backdrop, he was sharing the hillside home he had purchased in 1980 with Farida and Amalonda. How had this come about? It happened so fast. The settled world he had known in Soweto had been overturned by his accidental meeting with Bertha in the pharmacy.

That day, back in William's Nancefield apartment, Bertha had accepted his lifesaving offer—a new life in Zambia not only for herself but for little Amalonda, as well. But with a condition, he had said: Never to speak about what took place in 1998. It was to forever remain locked in the attic of the past. Or so Bertha thought.

Puffing away on his pipe, William's cheeks glowed with happiness as he watched Bertha and Amalonda down below. Their shirts were tucked high as they held hands while wading in a water garden splashed with colorful aquatic plant life. The sound of their playful laughter drifting toward him was music to his ears. His heart skipped a beat. Could Bertha ever feel the way he did for her? William sighed. Thirty-five years was quite an age gap for a woman, let alone one who had just recently thrown away her nun's habit. Would she reject the love that, at this moment, was overpowering him?

Even though he met her when her beauty was masked by contusions and bruising, William had never forgotten the face of the most beautiful woman he had ever seen. Nor could he deny that he had wanted to be her knight in shining armor that fateful day—to whisk her away from the hellhole of Samuel's apartment and into the sunset. Even when their paths had briefly crossed in the Soweto Infirmary, Bertha was all he thought about. Now he *was* her knight, and deep down he hoped that time would make Bertha understand that he loved her and would lay down his life for her.

William was older and wiser now, and he had more than enough patience and willingness to try to make Bertha his third wife, and to adopt Amalonda as his daughter. He was aware that this procedure would not be easy. The child had literally been "removed" from Soweto without receiving consent from her relatives. They would need to present police records, medical records and three personal references from friends in order to begin adoption proceedings. An assigned social worker would be brought into the picture, and if everything went smoothly, there would be a court appearance.

Could it happen?

Absolutely. William wasn't without professional and legal connections.

Was it in the best interest of the girl?

Absolutely.

Apart from the Christmas gifts showered on Amalonda when she arrived at her new home, he was the best gift she could receive—a hands-on father who loved her as his own.

Amalonda's health was improving daily, kept in check by William, and the adoption papers filed in the court were awaiting the judge's final review. In the meanwhile, she continued to call Bertha "Mum" and William "Daddy Will." She attended a local school and instantly had become the teacher's pet.

In January of 2010, life in the Ungobo household was idyllic— perfect harmony reigned within the walls of the happy home. Not long after Amalonda started attending the local school, Bertha, whose scoliosis was also kept in check by William, applied for a teaching position at the same school and was accepted. William, feeling somewhat at a loose end with his "family" gone all day, offered his services at a small, local clinic nearby. There, the high number of teen pregnancies kept him busy. Bertha was therapeutically occupied. William was doing what he did best— saving lives. And Amalonda was excelling educationally. William the family man was complete.

Late one night, in the beginning of February, William's beeper went off. He hurriedly answered the callback.

"Doctor, could you please come right away," the duty nurse requested. "It's urgent. We have a young mother from the Congo who is in labor. I'll explain the difficulties we are having when you get here. Could you hurry, please?"

Bertha awoke to the sounds of William's bedroom door closing nosily. She hurriedly put on a robe. When she learned of the urgency at the hospital, she offered to drive William in the brand new Volvo he had purchased for her.

Parked outside the medical building, Bertha turned to William. "Call me when you are done, and I'll come and get you. Or would you like me to wait here for you?"

"No, thanks, dear heart," he replied. "You go and get some sleep. You have class tomorrow. I'm sure I can get a ride home."

Bertha smiled inwardly. He was such a kindhearted man, always considerate of others. However, she did have reservations about the constant endearments he threw her way on a daily basis. Yet, coming from this gentle giant of a man, the words were flattering. Oh, she wasn't hiding behind a wall. She knew that his intentions, although honorable, were calculated for much more. But she wasn't ready to have a relationship with him, or any man, for that matter. No. She was damaged goods and nothing could persuade her otherwise. Their platonic friendship was working well. Or so she thought.

Bertha drove home, smiling.

In the clinic, the nurse pulled back the curtain. There, writhing in agony and crying on the birthing bed, was a dark-skinned girl whose panicked eyes now focused on William. He thought he had seen it all, but here was a girl who didn't look much older than Amalonda. He turned to the nurse. "How old is she?"

"She doesn't know for sure, but her father's outside in the waiting room. Do you want me to find out?"

The doctor sighed. He was well aware that this small, ill-equipped infirmary—a far cry from his private medical clinic in Nairobi, or more recently, the Soweto hospital—wasn't as up to date in lifesaving technology or nursing training as he would have liked. Nevertheless, not getting information about a patient beforehand was inexcusable.

William approached the girl, who immediately shrunk under her covering sheet. "It's okay," he soothed. "I'm here to help you. What's your name?"
Silence.

"How old are you?" He stopped himself from asking a normal medical question: "Is this your first baby?" It was obvious that she was a child having a child.

Silence.

William pulled the overhead exam light into position, dragged the cart with the fetal monitoring device closer, and then gently coaxed the sheet from the terrified girl's grip. Again he gently said, "You are going to be okay. I'm going to take good care of you and your baby."

Only the sound of her heavy, labored breathing was returned. He donned surgical gloves and gently parted her legs. "Oh, dear Lord above!" his head screamed. It had been a while since he had been witness to something so horrendous. Not only was the poor girl circumcised, her clitoris missing, but her labia minora (genitalia lips) was stitched over the opening to her vagina. The only way birth was possible was to surgically undo this barbaric practice. If he did not, he could lose both mother and child. William wasn't going to let that happen.

The night nurse who had gone after information returned saying, "Doctor, I had a bad time trying to get anything from her father. He only speaks a Congo dialect, but I managed to get through to him with hand gestures. His daughter's name is Suni, and she is eleven. And this comes as no shock to me ... he is the father of her baby!"

William didn't show his emotions, but inside he was madder than an angry wasp. He had to put his disgust behind him and save his patient and her baby's life.

A half-hour later an emergency C-section was performed, but it was too late for the premature baby girl. William and the night staff did everything they could to save this tiny baby's life, but she failed to intake breath. And to make matters worse, Suni let out her last breath a few minutes after the baby was removed. William had frantically tried to resuscitate her. With the naked eye, he couldn't see the medical reason for her sudden death. Part of him believed that it was God's hand, that *He* had taken this poor abused girl to a better place.

William wanted to knock the head off her father when the elderly man wanted to know if she had given birth yet. William didn't waste his breath on this lowlife. Instead, he lifted the telephone receiver and dialed. "This is Dr. William Ungobo at Mercy Hospital. I would like to report the rape of a child."

William's fists were balled as he watched the police cart the despicable man away. Why hadn't he done the same when Samuel had broken the law? William didn't have an easy answer. Exhausted and heartbroken, William hitched a ride home with an off-duty policeman.

Back in the quiet of his home, William broke down. He wept like a baby. Bertha, who had been waiting up for him, rushed to the easy chair where he was slumped. She wrapped her arms around him and whispered in his ear, "I'm here for you. What's happened? Do you want to talk about it?"

They clung to each other, drenching themselves in unspeakable sorrow for the demise of the girl and her unborn baby. After a short while, regaining her composure, Bertha said softly, "We are living in a world of moral decay, and I truly believe that nothing can be done about it."

William nodded. "I know. But God has a plan for us."

Bertha straightened her back, and a deluge of bitterness spewed forth. "God does nothing about mankind's sick-minded practices. Did he *remove* the slave yokes and chains from our people? Set them free? Did he strike down the slavers? No, they prospered. Did he strike down evil tyrants who caused world wars? No. He *allowed* Hitler to thrive and murder six million Jews! And you asked me why I don't go to church with you. Well, I think you have your answer. There is no God!"

"Oh, dearest Bertha, if that's the way you feel, I will not try to change your mind. But it is my strongest desire to marry you and have a proper church wedding. Will you consider it?"

William could have floored her with a feather.

Bertha fled the living room in the same haste she'd made after sister Anne had offered her a glass of lemonade so long ago.
In the solace of her bedroom, with her face smack in her pillow, the cushion darkness could not erase the face looming toward her."No! Please stop, Father Samuel ..."

Her scream was louder than any birthing scream.

It was William's turn to comfort her. He rocked her in his arms. He knew that no words could heal her internal scarring. She had been marked for life. And his blood was to blame. But the healer inside William was not going to give up. He would sacrifice his life to erase her "old" life. He had never felt such overwhelming love for a woman. Farida was, indeed, "special" in his eyes.

But Fate had already sealed Bertha's life the day she found Shiya's jewels.

One morning, a month and a half after the young girl and her baby died, Amalonda found Bertha floating face down in the pond. Stuck to Bertha's knotty hair was an eagle feather.

Trying to cast off the haunting legacy of three major traumas— the circumcision, the village massacre, and the excruciatingly painful rape—and then pulling away from her "put-on" religion and its severe disciplinary rules, had taken the spunk out of *who* Bertha really was—a little girl named Farida.

With her scars far too deep, she had gone to the pond in the middle of the night wearing only Shiya's well-worn sandals. There, she turned her head heavenward and spoke to the still night air. "There are no keys to unlock the door to the fragility of my human life, which now is but embers of a dying soul that even love can't reignite. I have endured the life you gave me, Lord, not knowing if love or hope existed."

She threw herself into the deep pond, and before she breathed the cold water of death into her lungs, she mouthed these words: "Yea, though I walk through the valley of the shadow of death, I will fear no evil ..."

At the very same time Farida's spirit soared heavenward, Mandegizi's heart stopped while he was climbing into his excavator. His sudden death was baffling, to say the least. Why had this young, healthy man succumbed to heart failure? According to his distraught wife, for the last little bit, Mandegizi had been experiencing heart throbs, and he felt his days were numbered—marked for death by the "rightful" owners, the spirits of the underworld, for his involvement in retrieving Shiya's buried jewelry.

And not that far from the dead machine operator, Zepsiweli lay dead—shot to death in a drive-by shooting on his way back from the local pub.

Shiya's "cursed" jewelry had kept its promise.

Unbeknown to the three people who had gone in search of the buried treasure, Sliman, the Tswanas witch doctor, had helped Shiya bury the tea caddy the day before he shot her. He had left the little people from the underworld as guardians. They were to be released when he recovered *his* fortune. Too bad—too late. Sliman never got the opportunity to recover his fortune. He was hanged in 1999.

Everyone who had touched these cursed jewels was gone.

Wrong!

There would be one more unsuspecting "cursed" soul.

"When you dance with the devil ..."

CHAPTER EIGHTEEN

Siavonga, Republic of Zambia, mid-February 2010

"Absent in body, but present in spirit."
—CORINTHIANS 5:3

AT THE BREAKFAST TABLE a month before the drowning, William and Bertha had hardly spoken to each other. William's sincere marriage proposal two weeks earlier had not touched Bertha the way it should have. Now, Amalonda broke the tension in the dining room. "I can't wait to get to school today," she gushed. "We are going on a field trip. I'm going to learn about plants, insects, and other amazing things."

"That's absolutely wonderful," Bertha and William responded in unison. Bertha added, "I'm looking forward to you coming home and telling us all about your day. But you had better hurry. The school bus will be here soon, so finish your breakfast. Then off you go."

Bertha just adored her talkative, intelligent daughter. In their short adjustment period as a family in Zambia, Amalonda was bubblier than she had ever been. She never mentioned her previous home in Soweto, her grandmother Umia, her awful drunken relatives, or anything else about her previous existence. Nor did she mention her episode with the ethereal Shiya. It was as if she had wiped the slate clean and was starting her life all over again. What made Bertha most happy was that Amalonda's HIV was under control. And later today, after the field trip, mom and daughter were looking forward to meeting the social worker assigned to them. That meeting was going to be the icing on the cake—the final adoption preparations.

At 4:30 P.M. Melissa Lusakanani knocked on the porch door. She was a big woman in her late forties, and she was intrigued by this particular assignment. She had never had a case that involved a doctor, an ex-nun, and a child who had no official birth certificate or registered last name. The girl was simply known as Amalonda of Soweto Township.

Bertha opened the door. "Good afternoon," she greeted. "You must be the case worker. Please come in," she invited. After the two women shook hands, Bertha led Melissa into the living room where William was waiting.

After the customary introductions, Melissa got down to business. "Is Amalonda here?"

"Not yet. But I'm expecting her home around five o'clock. She is on a field trip outing," Bertha replied.

Melissa opened her briefcase, pulled out a thin file folder, and said, "I must admit that this is a very unusual case. I'm hoping both of you can shed some light on it."

As the story unfolded, Melissa interrupted her absorbed silence with occasional "oohs" and "ahs." She continued listening attentively to William and Bertha's accounts of how seven-year-old Amalonda came to be in their care, how she could never be returned to her former drunken household, how she would be better off in her current stable environment, and how her precarious health would continue to be stabilized by William.

Melissa didn't wait for Amalonda to return. She went to her office and spent the next couple of hours writing her report.

Ten days later, a Zambian judge granted William and Bertha full custody of Amalonda. She was now officially their daughter. The family celebrated at one of Lusaka's finest restaurants.

Amalonda, wearing a new dress especially bought for the occasion, glowed with happiness. "Thank you Mum and Dad for saving me. I promise you, I'll be the best daughter ever."

William and Bertha had tears in their eyes as she spoke.

Bertha proudly said, "We couldn't have asked for a more special angel sent from heaven to be our loving daughter."

"Yes. You are our angel," William added with his own big, proud smile.

Life was good for this new family until the unforeseen tragedy struck.

After the drowning, life had taken on a new meaning; both William and Amalonda suffered holes in their hearts that were too big to be fixed. And in the years to come, they would cling to each other as if their lives depended on each other.

Amalonda would go on to reach great academic heights with the additional help of a stranger, another human being whom Amalonda never could have guessed cared about her. And some non-earthly persons cared about her, as well: Bertha and her mother, Nthara; Anele and her father, Naboto; and Shiya. All smiled down on her from heaven.

CHAPTER NINETEEN

Solicchiata, Sicily, June 30, 2010

"MAMA, WAKE UP!" Alberto Jr., age eleven, cried. The handsome little boy placed both hands on his mother's back and shook her hard. "Mama, wake up. It's nine o'clock. I'm going to be late for soccer practice."

Brianna opened her bloodshot eyes, made an ouch-my-head-hurts grimace, and slurred, "Oh, honey, Mama has a bad headache. Ask Father Risso to take you, or one of the servants. Mama wants to sleep."

With a sad, drawn face, Alberto said, "Mama, he's not a priest anymore. He's my dad. And he's not here. Have you forgotten that he is visiting his sick uncle in Torino?"

Brianna's alcohol blackouts were impacting her son and everyone else who resided at the Genovese mansion. How had this once pampered child, bright law student, and proud mother of twins fall down this dark, slippery slope?

In this picture-perfect, opulent setting, the bygone Genovese curse of misfortune that befell all the owners of this majestic home, had most definitely reawakened. The demons of alcohol were hard at work. The Brianna of late could kill off a box of wine by herself, but she didn't drink for pleasure. She drank to drown out the past. She was a broken soul who didn't know how to heal herself ... how to let go of the pain left by the loss of her mother and the ghastly revelations she had bestowed upon her daughter. Brianna felt defensive about her mother's shocking disclosures. But what really broke Brianna was that she was unable to save her own daughter, who had been diagnosed with childhood schizophrenia at age five. The power of a mother's love couldn't make it all go away because little Angelina was *lost*, hopelessly locked inside herself in the hallucinatory world of imaginary animals. She lived in a residential psychiatric care-treatment facility in Palermo. It was the final chapter of Brianna's meltdown. And so, alcohol became her savior.

Now, at age thirty-five, Brianna had no clue that she had diminished capacity because of her drinking. She had displayed no leadership and had no boundaries. Recent disasters—a chimney fire, a wine cellar break-in, and a pool drowning of a six-week-old puppy that had strayed from the litter—were furthest from her sodden mind.

Alberto Junior, his jaw set and fists balled, thumped his feet and marched from the room.

Without a care in the world, Brianna went back to sleep. She didn't hear the repeated knocking on her bedroom door.

Francesca, Brianna's secretary and long-time servant, opened the heavy door and stepped in. She shook Brianna's bare shoulder. "Señora, please wake up."

It took several shakes by Francesco before Brianna finally

opened her bloodshot eyes. Waking up was not easy.

"What the hell, Francesca!"

"I'm sorry to disturb you, but the courier is at the door. He has a registered parcel that needs signing. It has 'urgent' written in red all over the package."

"Okay. Give me a minute and I'll be down."

The courier stared at the dishevelled woman wearing a bright pink housecoat and matching slippers. Her eyes were so puffy she looked as if she hadn't slept in years.

After the necessary signature, Brianna stared at the well-parceled box. Then she noted the sender's name—"Miguel Rodriguez"—and address, and she frowned. She had seen neither hide nor hair of her mother's former attorney since their cantankerous meeting in the Palermo hospital after the birth of her twins. She vigorously shook her head as if trying to dispel that memory.

Taped to the inside of the box was a note dated 5 May 2010:

Hi, Brianna,

> *I hope you and your children are well and happy. And I would like to take this opportunity to say congratulations on your marriage to John Risso. It came as a big surprise!*

> *The reason I'm writing to you is that in late January of this year I received an e-mail from Winston Mandekana, who lives in London, England. I don't know if you remember him. He was the crime reporter who exposed the shootings of your mother and Anele back in 1998. Winston informed me that he had received correspondence from Sister Bertha, a Catholic nun, who asked him if he knew your whereabouts. He wrote back saying that he didn't know where you were living but that he would check it out.*

> *Shortly after Winston's e-mail, I telephoned Bertha at the*

number given in her correspondence to him and gleaned that she
wanted to return to you some items belonging to your mother. So
I instructed her to send them to me. They are now duly enclosed.

Take care and hugs to the twins.

If you need anything, you know where to find me.

Mike.

When Brianna opened the rusty old tea caddy and spilled out its contents, she couldn't believe her eyes. She was staggered. One particular piece of jewelry caused her to swallow hard. She picked up the gold locket and opened the delicate catch. "Oh, my God!" she exclaimed. The tiny swatch of colorful material that her mother had ripped off Anele's skirt before they were brutally separated on the Hallworthy estate back in 1950 was undamaged.

With her sober heart now heavy with remorse, Brianna began to cry. She looked heavenward and softly said, "Mama if you can hear me, I'm so sorry for everything. Can you forgive me from beyond the grave? I'll have your remains brought back, and I'll bury you with your mother, Sofia, and your father, Alberto. I've been such a bitch. Can you ever forgive me?"

Calling Brianna had been an embittered woman was an understatement, even though her rage was a response to hurt and injury. Even so, she now realized she had to make a 180-degree turn if she was going to make it—if she was going to begin to unload the burden that had begun to destroy her character.

She had always been a mixture of a lion and lamb, highly spirited and yet extremely vulnerable. After her mother's death, she had turned herself into a monster—sentencing herself to a punishing life, one in which she found solace in alcohol. Brianna bobbed her head knowingly as she accepted this fact. With the necklace still clasped in her hand, she spurred herself into action. She lifted the telephone receiver and dialed. A deep voice on the other end answered, "This is Doctor Ungobo."

"Hi. I have no idea what time it is over there, so I hope I'm not waking you. My name is Brianna Risso, and I'm looking for a nun named Sister Bertha. Would you know how I could get in touch with her?"

"Are you a fellow nun?"

"I'm not a nun, but I regard myself as a friend. You see, I met Sister Bertha at Anele's funeral. I don't know if you are familiar with that name, but she and my mother were shot in a Zulu kraal back in 1998."

William took a deep breath. He was well acquainted with Anele and Shiya. Bertha often spoke about them, as well as the other women she had loved in Tswanas. What this foreign-sounding woman calling at 11:00 A.M. wanted was beyond reach, and he was forced to be the bearer of the bad news. "I'm sorry to inform you, but Bertha is no longer with us. She died this past March."

"Oh, I'm sorry to hear that."

"But she has a daughter. Her name is Amalonda. Would you like to talk to her?"

Brianna was stunned. "She has a *daughter*! But she's a nun!"

"Ah, it's a long story. Hang on a minute. I'll get Amalonda."

Amalonda and Brianna had a long, tearful telephone conversation. It ended with, "As soon as I can, I will come to see you. I promise."

"I'm looking forward to meeting you and the twins," Amalonda said sincerely.

"Can't wait," Brianna ended.

But as the saying goes: *Be careful what you wish for ...*

-The End-

About the Author

Lucia Mann is a former British journalist and the author of two previous African-set novels devoted to slavery and racial prejudice, *Beside an Ocean of Sorrow* and *Rented Silence* (CBC Book Award winner). Born in British Colonial South Africa in the wake of WWII, Mann saw and felt firsthand the pain and suffering of those who were treated as inferior because of the color of their skin. She currently resides in British Columbia, Canada, where she is fine-tuning her next novel, *The Smoldering Fire of the Unforgiving*.

Visit www.LuciaMann.com for more information on how you can help alleviate the scourge of modern-day slavery.

Made in the USA
Charleston, SC
30 July 2013